GEORGE MACKAY BROWN

George Mackay Brown (*1921–96*) was one of the twentieth century's most distinguished and original writers. His lifelong inspiration and birthplace, Stromness in Orkney, moulded his view of the world, though he studied in Edinburgh, and later under Edwin Muir at Newbattle Abbey College. From 1941 onwards he battled tuberculosis, and increasingly lived a reclusive life in Stromness, but despite his poor health he produced a regular stream of publications from 1954 onwards. These included *Loaves and Fishes* (1959), *A Calendar of Love* (1967), collections of short stories *A Time to Keep* (1969) and *Hawkfall* (1974), a widely read novel *Greenvoe* (1972), *Time in a Red Coat* (1984) and a steady output of prose and poetry, notably the novel *Beside the Ocean of Time* (1994), which was shortlisted for the Booker Prize and winner of the Saltire Book of the Year. His work is permeated by the layers of history in Scotland's past, by quirks of human nature and religious belief, and by a fascination with the world beyond the horizons of the known.

He was honoured by the Open University and by Dundee and Glasgow Universities. The enduringly successful St Magnus Festival of poetry, prose, music and drama held annually in Orkney keeps his memory alive and is his lasting memorial.

GEORGE MACKAY BROWN

A Calendar of Love
and other stories

This edition published in Great Britain in 2006 by
Polygon, an imprint of Birlinn Ltd
West Newington House
10 Newington Road
Edinburgh
EH9 1QS

www.birlinn.co.uk

ISBN 1 904598 73 0
EAN 978 1 904598 73 2

First published in 1967 by The Hogarth Press

British Library Cataloguing-in-Publication Data
A catalogue record for this book is available on request from the
British Library

The publisher acknowledges subsidy from

towards the publication of this volume

Typeset by Hewer Text UK Ltd, Edinburgh
Printed and bound by CPD (Wales) Ltd

For Pamela

Contents

Foreword   ix

A Calendar of Love   1

Five Green Waves   33

The Three Islands   53

The Seller of Silk Shirts   65

The Wheel   69

The Troubling of the Waters   75

The Ferryman   79

The Storm Watchers   85

Tam   93

Witch   97

Master Halcrow, Priest   117

The Ballad of the Rose Bush   129

Stone Poems   135

The Story of Jorkel Hayforks   139

Foreword

Orkney is a small green world in itself. Walk a mile or two and you will see, mixed up with the modern houses of concrete and wood, the 'old farmhouses sunk in time'; hall and manse from which laird and minister ruled in the eighteenth century; smuggler's cave, witch's hovel; stone piers where the whalers and Hudson's Bay ships tied up; the remains of pre-Reformation chapel and monastery; homesteads of Vikings like Langskaill where Sweyn Asleif-son wintered, the last and greatest of them all; the monoliths of pre-history; immense Stone Age burial chambers where the Norse Jerusalem-farers broke in and covered the walls with runes.

Dominating all the islands is the rose-red Cathedral of Saint Magnus the Martyr in Kirkwall, called 'the wonder and glory of all the north'.

This Magnus was a twelfth-century Earl of Orkney, in a time of terrible civil war. One April morning he heard Mass in the small church of Egilsay; then he walked out gaily among the ritual axes and swords. Next winter the poor of the islands broke their bread in peace.

Round that still centre all these stories move.

G.M.B.

A Calendar of Love

The fisherman Peter lived in a tarred hut above the rocks with his boat, his creels, his Bible.

Jean Scarth lived with her father (men called him Snipe) in the pub at the end of the village. Snipe lay in bed now all the time. The doctor said he would never see another New Year.

Thorfinn Vik the crofter lived in a new wooden house at the edge of the moor. His father and mother were dead now. His married sister lived in Canada.

*

Jean opened the pub at six o'clock. Peter was standing outside with three haddocks in his hand. He didn't come in, he gave Jean the fish and walked off into the darkness. He had his black suit on, the one he wore to the gospel meetings.

Thorfinn came at half past six. His face was gaunt and grey after the New Year drinking. He asked for beer and stood over the counter drinking it. Other men from the hill came in. Seatter of Stark and Eric Weyland came in and began to play draughts. Three tinkers came in.

Jean said to Thorfinn, 'Peter from the shore was here tonight. He's a good man, that.'

'Give me a whisky,' said Thorfinn. 'I must keep my strength up for the ploughing.'

'He had three fish but he never uttered a word,' said Jean.

The men from the hill went out, then the tinkers. Seatter of Stark and Eric Weyland sat over the draught-board.

Thorfinn said, 'The croft's still empty, up by.'

Jean said, 'I have a pub to work and a sick man to nurse. I can't come.'

'I love thee well,' said Thorfinn.

'And I think well of you,' said Jean. 'But I think little of your drinking and carry-on.'

Seatter of Stark and Eric Weyland began to grumble at each other over the draughtboard.

'It's past nine,' said Jean. 'Drink up and go.'

Thorfinn finished his whisky and went out. After a time Jean followed him to the door. The black footprints went off into the snow-brimmed village.

From the door of the Mission Hall opposite Peter stood watching her. The prayer meeting was over. His black Bible was in his hand.

FEBRUARY

After the gale in the second week of February there was much sea for days. Peter sat over his stove with the evangelical magazines. The ten lost tribes of Israel were not lost at all! They were here, in the islands of Britain, and Peter was one of them, Peter was an Israelite! He read on and on.

*

The van cost Thorfinn fifty pounds second-hand. Now he could go to dances in the farthest parishes and see new women. He had not passed the driving test, he had neither licence nor insurance, but he took the risk, driving at night, with no L-plates.

*

The old man, who had been so patient and carefree since he took to his bed, now began to summon Jean a hundred times a day. She would have to leave her beer-tap running and go up to him. He had become like a child. He wept and prayed in the darkness . . . 'Don't bury me beside Mary Ann,' said Snipe, 'nor yet beside my father and mother. There must be a new grave, and I want a granite stone with an anchor on it.'

*

Thorfinn was in the bar. 'A sheep was run over, up for Birsay the way, last night. It was me,' he said. 'If the police come, you must say I was here, alone in the parlour, drinking till closing time.'

'I won't tell them any such thing,' said Jean. 'That would be a lie.'

'There's a well-liked lass in Birsay,' said Thorfinn. 'I saw her last week at the dance. Sadie Flett, that's her name.'

'I wish you luck of her,' said Jean, 'and would you drink up, for it's closing time.'

The thin cry came from upstairs: 'Jean . . . Jean . . .'

*

At midnight the old man was still not sleeping. He was remembering ships and men from sixty years ago, and every memory was a torture.

'For God's sake and for God's sake go to sleep,' whispered Jean against the wall, 'for the strength and the patience are nearly out of me.'

There was a gentle knock at the outer door. Peter stood there in the moonlight.

'I saw the light in your father's room,' he said.

'He's far from well,' said Jean. 'The old bad things are troubling him.'

'I'll sit with him till the morning,' said Peter.

The night passed.

In the morning Jean found them as she had left them at midnight, Peter awake in the chair and Snipe in bed, but sleeping now as quiet as a stone.

'A morning for haddocks,' said Peter. 'I'll sleep in the afternoon. I'll watch again tonight . . . And as for thee,' he went on, 'thu must get out in the fresh air. Thu're as pale as a candle.'

MARCH

'I love thee,' said Thorfinn, 'I love thee well.'

'I love thee too,' said Jean.

Through the van window was the island of Gairsay, and birds, and a flowing sea. It was a Sunday evening – the police were presumably all at home.

The last of winter, a hard grey lump of snow, blocked the ditch. Silently, imperceptibly, the little rill of ditch-water unwove the stubborn snow, carried it off, a cold shining music, down to the loch and the swans.

For a long time they did not speak.

*

'Throw everything . . . all thy sins . . . thy weaknesses . . . in the arms . . . of the eternal . . . the everlasting . . .' said Peter earnestly and hopelessly over the shape in the bed.

'No, but listen,' said Snipe. 'It was in Montevideo they all got drunk and the next morning the skipper mustered the crew and eight were missing and the same morning the South American police came aboard and said they had seven of them in jail and to bail them out would cost a hundred and eight quid so the skipper—'

'Mr Scarth,' said Peter, 'O man, you're *dying*. Are you not sorry before Almighty God?'

'—because he *had* to sail,' said Snipe, 'that very day. So he paid up, or rather the consul paid. And it was a month before Jock Slater was dragged out of the harbour. He was the eighth one but they didn't have to pay a penny for him—'

'Listen,' cried Peter, 'in Revelation it says—'

But soon Snipe was out on his own, in a place beyond scriptures and seaports and bad foreign hooch.

*

Peter met Jean on the stair, 'Thy father's dead,' he said.

Later, beside the fire, he said, 'Bury thy father and sell this bad place. I love thee.'

'You're a good man, Peter,' said Jean.

She went once more to look at the dead face. She came back crying. 'O Thorfinn,' she said.

'Thorfinn!' said Peter. 'Do you want that badness all over again? Your father died speaking of drink. God help him, that's the truth. Do you want to go on living that way?'

'No,' said Jean, 'and you're a good man.'

'Do you want to go on staying in this place?' said Peter.

'No,' said Jean, and kissed him gently. And again.

He took her in his hard religious arms.

In the grey of morning Peter went out and knocked at the undertaker's door and went on home.

He went down on his knees among the nets and oars, and prayed.

APRIL

A stone went up in the churchyard:

In memory of
JOHN SCARTH
Inn-Keeper in this Parish
Formerly a Seaman
1880–1962

'May There Be No Moaning At The Bar
When I Put Out To Sea'

Carved anchors, dolphins, waves, sailing ships, tumbled after each other round the edge of the white marble.

'There should have been barrels of sour beer too, and naked women,' said Thorfinn.

And later he said, 'Many a poor bloody drunkard's last shilling went to pay for that stone.'

And to Jean he said, 'It's a credit to you, the stone you put up to Snipe . . .'

'Where are you going in the van tonight?' said Jean.

'Nowhere,' said Thorfinn.

'Tell me,' said Jean, 'so I won't need to hear it from the gossip-mongers.'

'I'm going to Holm,' said Thorfinn.

'To Hazel Groat,' said Jean.

Thorfinn drank his whisky down and went out.

*

Peter didn't come near the village now, not even for the gospel meetings. He bought his provisions from the grocery van.

'That's a fine stone they've raised for Snipe Scarth in the kirkyard,' said Josiah of the Shore to Peter across a black stretch of net.

'I never saw it,' said Peter.

'Tell me now,' said Josiah, 'would you say Snipe's in Heaven or in Hell?'

'It's not for me to say,' said Peter.

'Just so,' said Josiah. 'Poor man . . . And he has a daughter.'

'He has,' said Peter.

'The business is being carried on,' said Josiah. 'She has a sharp tongue in her head, that one. She'll comb the head of some poor man. Ay.'

'There's another tear in the net,' said Peter. 'What's needed here is a good woman that knows how to mend things, and to clean and to cook. The price of a good woman is above rubies . . .'

MAY

Jean, dreaming, walked on a green hill. There were swans in the water below her, and clouds like swans in the sky above.

A man walked along the road from the sea. He was all wet from a shipwreck. 'Gideon's fleece is not more glorious,' Peter said (for it was Peter). He was walking not towards her but towards Thorfinn, who was having difficulty in ploughing a field with the axle of a car.

Thorfinn turned and hewed at Peter with his plough-axle but it buckled on Peter's shoulder like cardboard. He touched Thorfinn with his black book. Formally, gently, Thorfinn fell across the furrow.

Jean was carrying a vase. She knelt to put it in a small grave in the corner of the field but a bird looked out of it, a blue bird with sweet frightened eyes. She gathered it in her hands. Its wings were cold. It was a bird of ice.

She was going into a church with a broken arch, where a service was going on. It was night. Her hands were cut and bleeding – inside she would find a cure. O, her hand was a thorn, a flame, such agony! Peter in a black cloak stood at the arch. He looked at her with blank eyes.

Farther in, hidden from her, voices were singing among cold, bright images.

Jean woke with a cry in the dawn.

*

Peter was walking down the beach, loaded with creels, towards his dinghy. Josiah walked five paces behind him, loaded with creels. It was a good morning for the lobsters.

*

All that month Thorfinn's van had been probing in another direction, out towards Orphir. The girl there was called Myra Stanger. After the dance he had made her drunk with gin. She sat in the van beside him now, singing in an ugly slack way. Thorfinn drove fast, to be home before the police were stirring. 'I love thee,' he said to Myra.

At Glengoes he stopped the van. He climbed through a fence and came back later with a dead dangling chicken. He threw it in the back of the van. Myra was asleep. He drank some gin. Then he started the engine again and drove on into the growing light.

JUNE

Thorfinn said to Jean, 'Ann Johnston. And Sadie Flett. And Hazel Groat. And Myra Stanger. And Agnes Sinclair . . . But thee I love.'

Jean said to Peter, 'So now I see it was only to save the soul of a bad old man you came visiting here.'

Peter said to Thorfinn, 'Thu're a thing of lust and drunkenness, and I have a strong inclination to drag thee like a rat through the ditch. I can't find in my soul one drop of love for thee, not one, God help me.'

Thorfinn said to Peter, 'I'll give thee five shillings for that skate, for not only salted does skate put a powerful thirst in the throat, but boiled it sends a man raging after women in the darkness of night, both in dreams and in reality.'

Peter said to Jean, 'I'm a poor man but strong in my body. I believe my election is sealed. I pray that grace will fall on thee also. I wish to see no woman but thee standing in my door every day when I haul the dinghy ashore after the fishing.'

Jean said to Thorfinn, 'This is what is wrong with me, this is why I have the darkness under my eyes and my mouth is full of sharp words, that I think I'm . . . O, go away . . . It's closing time!'

JULY

On the last day of the Carnival Week in Stromness, Thorfinn drove his unlicensed van past two policemen at the north end of the town and parked it in the square. In the Britannia Bar he drank whisky and beer. There were not many people in the town yet.

That day, Saturday, Peter did not go to the creels. In the afternoon he put on his white shirt and black suit. He took the Bible under his arm. He caught the bus to Stromness at the smithy.

Jean said to James Firth, 'I'll give thee a pound to serve at the bar tonight, and thu can have a double whisky before thu opens the door and another when the last customer has gone. Will thu do that? For I must go to Stromness . . .' James Firth agreed to do that, on those terms. Jean gave him the key.

*

Thorfinn left the Britannia Bar and went to the Hamnavoe Bar. He drank whisky. Andrew of Feadale came in. Andrew drank vodka, and stood Thorfinn a glass of vodka too. 'It has a queer taste, vodka,' said Thorfinn, 'like sweet paraffin, and the Russians must be a barbarous bloody nation to drink stuff like that' . . . Through the window they could see the parish buses coming in for the Carnival, one after the other.

Peter got off the bus and went to the house of William Simpson the butcher and evangelist. William Simpson did not believe that the British nation comprised the ten lost tribes of Israel. They argued the matter gravely over the ham-and-eggs, quoting texts and authorities. Afterwards they planned the order of the open-air service that was to take place at the Pierhead at seven o'clock, D.V.

Jean got off the bus and went to the doctor's surgery.

*

Thorfinn drank another glass of vodka with Andrew. Then he drank a glass of rum by himself, and then some whisky and beer. He bought a half-bottle of whisky and went back to the Britannia. There were many people in the street now. In the Britannia he met Sam of Biggings and Freddy and Jock and Archer and Tom.

Peter said to William Simpson that the New Dispensation of Grace began in the year 1917, on the day General Allenby walked into Jerusalem, as was abundantly proved by certain texts in Daniel and Revelation, namely . . . At this point, four more evangelists came in carrying Bibles.

Jean stood on one of the stone piers and watched the fishing boats riding at anchor. It was quiet here, and clean. The doctor had uttered six or seven words. It was lonely here. So the hunted animal carries her wound away to a secret water, and waits patiently for death or renewal.

*

Thorfinn drank whisky with the boys. The pub was so full now they decided to go through to the cocktail bar. The cocktail bar was full too. They stood against the wall and drank whisky. There were many girls in the cocktail bar. Freddy took a bottle of whisky out of his coat and passed it round the boys.

Peter stood with eleven others in a ring beside the fountain. They sang, 'Count Your Blessings', 'There is a Fountain', 'The Hallelujah Lifeboat'. Peter read out of Isaiah and Galatians. William Simpson preached. The Carnival – drunkenness, lechery, violence – raged all round that shining circle. Inside was Sion, the promise, the everlasting courts of the King.

The floats went by, one after another, bearing Stone Age men, mermaids, a surgical theatre, a shebeen, a school-room, Hell, a Turkish harem, a moon-ship. Then walking clowns, Hawaiian girls, Victorians, Cossacks, Red Indians, Chinamen, Martians. Jean stood in the door of the pharmacy and watched the procession cleaving the crowd, spreading behind a wide wake of cheers, shouts, ribaldry.

*

'I'll buy thee a drink. I love thee,' said Thorfinn at a table where two girls he didn't know and two young men were sitting.

'No,' said the girl.

Thorfinn fell across their table and slithered on to the floor in a ruin of gin and beer and broken glass.

Then he found himself outside.

He had never seen so many faces.

He fell on the street. Cars hooted all round. A great walking pelican straddled him.

'Anyone who thinks that is a fool,' said William Simpson. 'He is a liar and the truth is not in him.'

'*I* think that,' said Peter.

'Then,' said William Simpson severely, 'if the cap fits, you can wear it.'

They were having black puddings and tea in William Simpson's parlour after the open-air meeting.

From the street below came Carnival cries, songs, laughter, from the hordes of the lost.

'You would like to dictate. You think you have the

whole truth. In your pride you think you're God's chosen man in this island,' said Peter.

The ten other evangelists listened in a dark silence.

'If it comes to that,' said William Simpson with great deliberation, 'I have never consorted *with publicans and sinners*' . . . He munched at his bread. Three of the evangelists looked at Peter accusingly.

Nearly everybody on the street was drunk now. Jean struggled to get to the last bus through the ebbing crowds. She was desperately tired. Vivid images glowed and faded in her mind – three fish, a nautical gravestone, a winter cradle, a bird in a vase, Thorfinn at the plough, Thorfinn at the dart-board, Thorfinn helpless on a mad street . . .

Round the corner, near the bus stance, a jazz band began to play, and the coloured lights came on.

*

Thorfinn found himself at the wheel of his van. A strange girl was sitting beside him, stroking his head. How had he got here?

He kissed the girl.

He felt in his hip pocket for the whisky. It wasn't there.

'I'll drive thee home,' said Thorfinn.

'Yes,' said the girl. She went on combing his hair with her fingers.

Solemnly Thorfinn turned the van and drove through the crowd, out of the town.

The police sergeant was standing at the Bank gate. He

looked searchingly at Thorfinn. Solemnly and slowly
Thorfinn drove past him.

Peter, his Bible askew under his arm, hurriedly crossed
the street in front of the van. Thorfinn blasted him with
the horn.

'I love thee,' said Thorfinn to the girl. 'Where does thu
live?'

Peter, having missed the last bus, decided to walk
home.

He was finished with that crowd in Stromness. He
would never go to their meetings again. Never.

He could have taken William Simpson and broken him,
so angry had he been! . . . By God's help, he had managed
to control himself.

But this was the end. He had been to his last gospel
meeting in Stromness. Never again.

A green van careered past him.

As Peter walked home, the Carnival rockets rushed up
the darkening sky, one after another. Out of their ruin,
silent globes of light blossomed and floated, yellow and
green and red, to die suddenly on the midnight . . .

Jean took the key from James Firth and gave him a
pound. She locked the door and put out the light. Alone in
the darkness she felt for a moment she wanted to pray, but
she could think of nobody to pray for except the pelican
guiser who had lifted Thorfinn out of the gutter . . . and
maybe the burden inside her that already filled her with
such weariness and shame – the pilgrim – the stranger –
the lawless dancer.

AUGUST

Three among hundreds of advertisements one week in the *Orcadian*, the local newspaper:

THE TEN LOST TRIBES OF ISRAEL – *where are they?* They inhabit the British Isles *today*! We are THE CHOSEN PEOPLE in a world *hastening to its end*! Those who would like to know more about this *undoubted fact* are invited to a public meeting in Ingsevay Community Centre on (D.V.) 15 August, at 8 p.m.

Experienced full-time *barman* wanted for Ingsevay Inn. Wages £8 10*s.* per week. Apply Miss Jean Scarth, The Inn, Ingsevay.

FOR SALE – A green Morris van, 1945, in first-class running order. Can be seen. Apply Box No. 3124.

SEPTEMBER

The oatfield of Helliar was almost cut. Thorfinn had never been so tired. Since before dawn six of them, men and girls, had been working in the field. For this one harvest day the sun had stored up all the heat and glare of a dull summer. It burst suddenly out of the early morning mist and laid an unclouded flame on the hill-side. The wind and rain of the previous week had laid and tangled the corn, so that it was hard to cut. Girls and men toiled together, gathering and binding. The reaper jolted along like a huge clogged purposeful insect. About noon the men had taken off their shirts. Thorfinn's back, aflame with the sun, was mottled in addition with insect bites.

They ate their dinner under the south wall – chicken and bannocks and home-brewed ale.

'Where are the clouds of July and August?' said Thorfinn, taking his arm across his sweat-silvered brow. Sam cursed sun, oats, reaper, sweat, women, dogs, the Fall of Man. Ann and the other girls laughed, packing away the plates and bottles.

Thorfinn finished his ale and rose groaning into the hot blue afternoon. Freddy climbed once more into the reaper.

They moved forward, step by step. The corn fell with long hot sighs. The girls followed, gathering and binding the sheaves. The heat accelerated, the insects moved in from the heather. All afternoon the hillside was lapped by pitiless flame. But now at last the harvesters had found a perfect rhythm – faultlessly, effortlessly, they moved through the corn, stooping, rising, burdening and disburdening themselves as in some ritual of birth and death. Sun blistered, insects troubled and stung, limbs were heavy and sore, but the great shining ceremony went on through the afternoon. The bread and ale were secure for another year.

At six o'clock the field was all cut and the harvesters went home.

*

Peter was gathering limpets from the rocks at low tide, out beyond the Point of Ramness. Slowly he went along the beach, a tin pail in one hand and a blunt knocking-stone in the other. Slowly and surely he moved among the clusters of limpets, knocking them into his ringing bucket.

The tide was at full ebb, the beach was heaped with layer upon layer of tangle. And there, in those brown wastes, a sudden bright swathe!

He went nearer, keeping his balance with difficulty in the slippery weed.

It was long blonde hair.

Peter pulled back the mantling seaweed. A cold dead face looked up at him.

He stood among the seaweed, shocked . . . Who could it be? There was that paragraph in the *Orcadian* a fortnight ago about the Hoy woman who was missing . . . But could the sea have carried her over all this way, from Hoy? She was young.

Peter bent down and lifted her in his arms. Water slopped out of her clothes. Staggering, he carried her up the beach and laid her on a flat sloping rock. The sea streamed from her over the hot stone.

It was a long way from the tents in the deserts of Sinai to this salt pool. It was a long way from the terrible mercy of Jehovah to the wearing doubts and despairs of a corrupt perverse Godless generation.

He walked the mile back to the village. At the shop he got three pennies for a threepenny bit. He phoned the police at Kirkwall.

The body lay on the rock, guarded by a gull and a pail of limpets.

*

Up among the hills, seven miles from Ingsevay, the tinkers were sleeping in their tent.

'Would you stop muttering to yourself,' said old Ezra to the thin huddle beside him, 'and go to sleep.'

'I'm praying,' said Williamina, 'and don't say another word till I'm done.'

'What are you praying for when the hill's full of rabbits?' said Ezra.

'I'm praying for that girl Jean in Ingsevay. She's going to have a bairn. She's like a ripe apple. She's the shape of an egg.'

'Hurry up then,' said Ezra, 'for it's a hot night, and I want to sleep.'

Williamina asked the Virgin and St Magnus and all the other bright saints of Heaven to pray for Jean who had retreated into the darkness, out of folk's sight, with her precious shameful burden – Jean, who had always been good to the tinkers and given them beer and bread whenever they were passing through in the old poor destitute days before National Assistance.

She touched her crucifix among the straw and prayed for Jean.

'Who is the father of this child?' said Ezra in a sleepy voice.

'A man,' said Williamina.

She crossed herself, finishing her prayer. Then she slept.

OCTOBER

Peter hesitated, bit his lip, looked up and down the road and between the houses, then walked straight into the pub and up to the bar.

Seatter of Stark and Eric Weyland looked at him as if he were a ghost. So the elders might look at them some Sabbath morning, if ever they stepped doucely into the kirk.

'I want to speak to Miss Scarth,' said Peter to James Firth, who had been permanent barman now for two months.

'Jean's not seeing anybody,' said James Firth.

'Tell her *I'm* here,' said Peter.

'It wouldn't matter a damn if I told her the Archbishop of Canterbury or the Dalai Lama was here, she wouldn't see them,' said James Firth.

'Give me a piece of paper,' said Peter, 'I'll write her a note.'

Jean – from study of scripture and multiplying signs I make it that this world is near an end. Woe then unto them that have turned aside. It were better for them, etc. I desire to save thee.

This thy house Rimmon is a house marked for quick destruction.

Come to where I live beside the sea and thou shalt be looked after, both thee and thy unborn child. Tarry here and thou shalt taste of the bitterness of loss. I am thy servant, Peter.

Having folded it and handed it to James Firth for delivery, Peter went out again past those two gaping thirsts, Seatter of Stark and Eric Weyland.

He hadn't been gone five minutes when Thorfinn came in.

'Give me a pint,' said Thorfinn, 'and tell me am I in the horrors with drink, or did that holy fisherman, the damnation-monger, walk out of this place two minutes ago?'

'He did,' said Seatter and Eric together.

'It *must* be near the end of the world then,' said Thorfinn. To James Firth he said, 'I want to see Jean.'

James Firth said, 'She isn't seeing anybody.'

'Tell her it's me,' said Thorfinn.

'It wouldn't matter,' said James Firth, 'if you was Robbie Burns, Casanova and Don Juan all in one.'

'Let's see a piece of paper then,' said Thorfinn.

He wrote:

My dear Jean – I've said to a hundred lasses, one time or another, 'I love thee'. All lies. But to thee I say, 'I love thee' and 'I love thee' and 'I love thee', when will I see you? Thorfinn.

Upstairs Jean read the two letters and put them both on the fire. She tried to retrieve Thorfinn's but the flame beat her. Flake by black flake, they drifted up the chimney.

NOVEMBER

The first snowflake of winter.

At five past five, Josiah summoned up courage to say, 'I doubt, Peter, thu've made a miscalculation.'

In Peter's hut were gathered Josiah, Josiah's wife Bella, Josiah's cousin Hedda from the quarry, and Josiah's children Aaron and Rebecca. Aaron and Rebecca had been crying, their faces were stained with tears, but now they were quiet again, as if they realized that a great crisis was safely past.

Josiah began again, 'I doubt, Peter—'

'Yes,' said Peter sadly, 'you can all go home now.'

It was to have been the end of the world. Peter had calculated it as being due to take place at four-ten that afternoon, and so he had invited Josiah and his dependants (as well as several others who had not come) to assemble in his hut, to the end that all true believers in the parish might be together when the terrible and glorious event took place. But nothing had happened.

'It won't be today,' said Peter, and opened the door. 'I must have made a miscalculation.'

The two children ran shouting into the darkness.

Then the heavens did give a sign. As Peter stood in the lighted doorway, the sky opened and released the first snowflake of winter.

*

Thorfinn sold the van at last to a Kirkwall docker, and undertook to deliver it on Thursday afternoon at Kirkwall pier.

Unlicensed, uninsured, untested, Thorfinn climbed into the green van for the last time. (He had partially covered the number plates with a careless drapery of sacking.) The darkness was coming down.

At Kiln Corner, on the edge of Kirkwall, a policeman

flashed his torch at Thorfinn, signalling him to stop. Thorfinn pressed his foot on the accelerator. The van rushed forward. Sweating, Thorfinn turned it into Bridge Street, and eased it into the dark corner of the car park. He got out quickly, whipped the sacking from the number plates, and walked up Bridge Street and along Albert Street. There, opposite the Big Tree, the policeman was, and one of his colleagues with him. They were waiting for a green van to pass. Thorfinn endured their scrutiny and walked on. They hadn't recognized him.

He turned down Castle Street, along Junction Road, and walked down the long pier. There, loading barrels of whisky with a score of other dockers, was his man. Thorfinn told him where the van was parked, then walked back up the pier. The pubs were just opening. He drank three glasses of rum, and went home on the bus at half past six.

Agnes Sinclair was on the bus. She signalled to him, made room for him on her seat. He sat by himself in the front.

At the Dykes he got off the bus. He walked up the long miry road to Helliar. Beyond the peat-stack the police van was parked. When they saw Thorfinn coming the two policemen climbed out of their black van and the Kirkwall docker followed them.

The first policeman called to Thorfinn to stop.

Thorfinn stopped. His fists swelled in the pockets of his raincoat. Would he rush them now, or take them one by one at the gate?

The first snowflake of winter trembled in the air above

the henhouse. It eddied and shimmered in the wind. Then it fell lightly and sweetly on to Thorfinn's hot clenched fist, a kiss of peace.

Grinning, he walked forward to meet the interrogators.

*

Jean sat alone at the top window of the Ingsevay Inn. Through the window, the hill darkened. The sky was grey.

For four months she had lived in this room. She had neither shown herself outside nor in the bar below. She was dedicated to loneliness.

She sewed in a chair beside the window. She waited.

The days darkened round her.

In her womb the slow shameful inexorable dance went on.

But now the shame had died. She was simply indifferent. Indifference lay on her like a heavy stone.

Down below, an argument broke out. It flared, then faded into muttered imprecations and reproaches. Jean recognized the voices of Seatter of Stark and Eric Weyland. James Firth was not good at controlling such outbursts.

Let them carry on. She didn't really care now.

The hill darkened.

Suddenly she saw the first snowflake. It fluttered over the rose bush in the garden. It climbed the air, circled, meandered down the wind. Then surely, gently, chastely, it drifted on to the window and clung there, shimmering.

This was beautiful!

Startled, she looked at the frail grey thing on the windowpane. The dead stone lifted inside her.

And then suddenly everything was in its place. The tinkers would move forever through the hills. Men would plough their fields. Men would bait their lines. Comedy had its place in the dance too – the drinking, the quarrelling, the expulsion, the return in the morning. And forever the world would be full of youth and beauty, birth and death, labour and suffering.

The child moved inside her in a wind of light . . .

The snowflake lived on her window for five seconds, then died into a glistening drop of water.

The hill darkened. A hundred snowflakes fell, a thousand, the wind crammed them against the pane. The hill was lost.

Down in the bar the voices rose again, Seatter of Stark and Eric Weyland.

Jean went quickly downstairs and opened the door into the bar. They were arguing across a draughtboard. Eric screeched, Seatter growled, their flaming faces set close together.

'Out,' said Jean quietly, and pointed to the door.

They hastened to be gone, like men caught with their trousers down. They almost fell over each other in the door. They were gone.

The awkward silence lasted only for a second.

'Jean, lass,' said Sam of Biggings, 'we haven't seen thee this long while, and we've missed thee, and we're glad to see thee again.'

'And I'm glad to see thee, Sam,' said Jean. 'And thee,

Andrew. And thee, Freddy. And thee, Jock. And Ezra and Williamina from the hill . . . James,' she said to the barman, 'whisky on the house for all here, to warm us for the winter.'

Out on the road, Seatter of Stark was saying to Eric Weyland, 'That's the last drink I buy in that place.'

'The impudence, putting *us* out, her best customers!' said Eric. 'And her with that great pirate cargo in her!'

'A shameless slut!' said Seatter of Stark.

The cold wind blew them over the hill helter-skelter.

It was snowing faster now.

DECEMBER

'Turn her,' said Peter. Josiah leant on the tiller. A wave broke against the *Bethel*, involved them in its ruin, lurched on.

With the blizzard they could see nothing. They might be out in the Sound, they might be under the Black Crag, they might be among the Kirk Rocks.

The engine coughed and snored.

With the blizzard, wind and sea had risen. They were on a broken perilous stair, climbing and falling blindly.

'Watch this wave,' said Peter. The wave licked at them coldly, shrugged on.

'Is it an inshore wave, or a wave of the Sound?' said Peter.

'It's more of an inshore wave,' said Josiah. 'God preserve us.'

'Turn her,' said Peter. Josiah leant on the tiller. The *Bethel* slipped into a trough between green waves, shuddering.

'Steady,' said Peter. The second wave rolled over them, almost rolled them over. The boat took much water.

They could see nothing. Out of a circular wall of blackness the snow came at them, from all directions. Under the wild-woven shroud at the bottom of the boat there were shapes of fish. The oilskins of the men were black behind, white in front.

The engine coughed. Another salt spasm set the *Bethel* shuddering from stem to stern.

'Turn her,' said Peter.

Josiah leant on the rudder. 'I never wanted to come out this morning,' he said. 'It was foolishness.'

Peter, bent over the engine, said nothing.

'Now we're in God's hands,' said Josiah.

'What better hands could we be in?' said Peter.

A wave came at them. The *Bethel* rose against it. They met, coughing and snarling, tore each other, and passed on.

Peter's hands were blue, heavy, lifeless as he bent over the engine, probing. He didn't like the sound it was making. Maybe they would have to hoist the sail.

Snow came at them from all directions.

Josiah screamed, 'O Christ, a rock!'

The black rock rose twenty yards away. The sea was breaking white on it. It was Braga.

'Thank God,' said Peter. Now he knew exactly where they were. 'Turn her,' he said.

Josiah leant on the rudder. His face was a mask of snow.

A new wave threw them forward.

*

The village was isolated. Through four hushed days and nights the snow had fallen, and spread a vast monotony.

On the fifth day the wind got up. It worked on the blank parish and everywhere altered its contours. It laid white drifts across the roads into Ingsevay, it dragged down the telegraph wires, it buried folds and fences and fishing boats in the noust.

And still the snow fell.

Seatter of Stark and Eric Weyland went into the pub at noon. It was empty.

They stamped their feet and beat on the counter with their knuckles. Nobody answered.

They knew that James Firth would not be there, the roads were blocked. But where was Jean? The door was open. The fire was lit.

They set out the draughts on the window seat and waited.

Ezra and Williamina came in. Their faces shone for a minute in the open door, like people transfigured.

'Where's Jean?' said Williamina.

The draught-players shook their heads.

The tinkers stood at the fire, stamping their feet.

'I'll go and draw two pints,' said Ezra. 'We can pay when she comes in.'

'Maybe she's at the well,' said Eric Weyland.

Williamina said, when their glasses were half empty, 'Maybe her time's come.'

'Ah,' said Ezra, 'drink up. We'll have two more pints while we're waiting.'

Seatter of Stark heard the noise first, it came from

upstairs, a thin flutter and a cry, like a winged duck in a marsh. He said nothing, but his eyes bulged.

The noise came again, and this time they all heard it.

'It's Jean,' said Williamina.

Seatter of Stark and Eric Weyland knocked over the draughtboard in their hurry to be gone. They left the door swinging on its hinges. A flurry of snow wet the blue stone floor of the pub.

'We better get the doctor,' said Ezra, though he knew the telephone lines were down and the road was blocked.

'I've taken a hundred bairns into the world,' said Williamina. She drank off her beer and went upstairs.

Ezra shut the door and put the iron bar across it. He put three lumps of coal on the fire. Then he went behind the bar and lowered a singing rope from the brandy bottle into a half-pint glass.

*

Thorfinn woke late to find Helliar half buried in snow.

His throat was dry after the whisky last night with Sam of Biggings. He put on his coat and set off towards the village for beer.

Beyond Voar, the drifts were high. The road wandered away into a white blank.

He tried to get round by the field above, and came back half an hour later, sodden and red in the face.

He knocked on the window of Voar and asked for a shovel to clear a way through.

'The snow's too deep,' said Bella of Voar.

He dug for an hour into the towering whiteness and blankness . . . It was impossible.

The four spinsters of Voar called him in to drink tea.

'Ah,' said Maggie, 'and how much did they fine you in the Sheriff Court?'

'Fifty pounds,' said Thorfinn, 'with the option of three months' imprisonment. And I'm disqualified from driving for two years . . . To obstructing the police in the lawful exercise of their duty, charge not proven.'

They looked at him in reprobation and admiration, and put more scones and tea in front of him.

The women of Voar were plain and stout. None of them was ever married. Their names were Bella, Maggie, Betsy and Isa. They spoke in the old-fashioned way.

Thorfinn got to his feet. 'I must get through to the village,' he said.

'For drink?' said Isa disapprovingly.

'For drink,' said Thorfinn. 'Give me the shovel. I'll try once more.'

The snow had stopped now. He took the spade and went out again. Bella went to the henhouse. Maggie went to the byre. Betsy sat at the spinning wheel. Isa moved about the kitchen, between the fire, the cupboard, the table, seeing to the dinner.

The four women of Voar assembled for their soup at two o'clock. Through the window they could see a small black figure in the snow, like a wingless legless fly on a vast tablecloth.

He would never, never get through.

The spade was striking at the drift in a slow dull mechanical rhythm. Thorfinn was beaten. But he went on digging.

'No man digs like that for drink,' said Maggie.

'It's for the woman,' said Betsy.

'Yes,' said Isa, 'it's for Jean.'

'They say her time's near,' said Betsy, 'and the father is said to be that gospel fisherman Peter, but be that as it may, it's a good job old Snipe's lying in the kirkyard away from it all.'

Thorfinn was still digging. They watched him through the window with pity and amusement.

'The phone,' said Bella.

Betsy said, 'The line's down.'

'We can try,' said Isa.

Maggie dialled the Ingsevay Inn and got through at once. A drunk tinker voice spoke from the other end. Maggie couldn't make out what he was saying. Sometimes he sang. He mentioned trout and bagpipes. Finally he said, 'I'm drunk with the brandy.'

Maggie said severely, 'Please tell us how Jean is . . . Miss Scarth.'

'There's a new landlord at the Inn since an hour ago,' said the black reeling old voice, 'and may he grow up to be a kinder landlord . . . than old Snipe his grandfather . . . him that's lying out there in the kirkyard . . . under the falling snow . . . and never once in his life . . . gave a poor tinker . . . as much as a thimbleful. . . .' The voice died away into a long musical sigh. 'I'm drunk . . . with the brandy . . .'

Outside, Thorfinn was sitting on the edge of the drift, with the spade across his knees and his head in his hands. He was beaten. He would never get through.

They sent out Betsy to tell him the news. Bella raked the fire. Maggie took from the cupboard a full bottle of whisky and five glasses.

Five Green Waves

I

Time was lines and circles and squares.

'You will go home at once to your father,' said Miss Ingsetter, rapping her desk with a ruler, 'and tell him I sent you, because you have not prepared the mathematics lesson I told you to prepare. Now go!'

A rustle went through the class-room. The pupils looked round at me, wide-eyed. A few made little sorrowing noises with their lips. For it was a terrible punishment. My father was a magnate, a pillar of authority in the island – Justice of the Peace, Kirk Elder, Registrar, Poor Inspector, a member of the Education Committee itself. He was, in addition, the only merchant in the place and kept the shop down by the pier; even before I was born he had decided that his boy would be a credit to him – he would go to the university and become a minister, or a lawyer, or a doctor.

Now, this summer afternoon, while blue-bottles like vibrant powered ink-blobs gloried in the windows and the sun came four-square through the burning panes, my stomach turned to water inside me.

'Please, Miss Ingsetter,' I said, 'I'm sorry I didn't learn

the theorem. I promise it won't happen again. I would be glad if you punished me yourself.'

The bust of Shelley gazed at me with wild blank eyes.

Her spectacles glinted. Down came the ruler with a snap. 'You will go to your father, now, at once, and tell him of your conduct.'

The bright day fell in ruins about me. I crossed the floor on fluttering bare feet, and was soon outside.

'You, Willie Sinclair,' I heard her shouting through the closed door, 'stand up and give us the theorem of Pythagoras.'

A red butterfly lighted on my hand, clung there for a moment, and went loitering airily across the school garden, now here among the lupins, now there over the flowering potatoes, as if it was drunk with happiness and didn't know on what bright lip to hang next. I watched it till it collapsed over the high wall, a free wind-tipsy flower.

Inside the class-room, the formal wave gathered and broke.

'. . . is equal to the sum of the squares on the other two sides,' concluded Willie Sinclair in a sibilant rush.

'Very good, Willie,' said Miss Ingsetter.

Despised and rejected, I turned for home.

II

The croft of Myers stands beside the road, looking over the Sound, and the hill rises behind it like a swelling green wave. Sophie, a little bent woman, her grey shawl about her head, was throwing seed to the twelve hens.

She smelt me on the wind. 'Hello there,' she cried. I muttered a greeting.

She peered at me. 'And who might you be?' she said. I told her my name.

'Mercy,' she said, 'but you've grown.'

Our voices had roused the old man inside. He was suddenly at the door, smiling. Peter's face was very red and round. He had been a sailor in his youth. The backs of his hands, and his wrists, smouldered with blue anchors, blue mermaids, blue whales. 'Come in,' he cried.

It was like entering a ship's hold, but for the smells of peat and kirn and girdle. I breathed darkness and fragrance.

They ushered me to the straw chair beside the fire. I had hardly got settled in it when Sophie put a bowl of ale between my hands. The sweet heavy fumes drifted across my nostrils.

Peter sat filling his pipe in the other straw chair. The old woman never rested for an instant. She moved between the fire and the window and the bed, putting things in order. She flicked her duster along the mantelpiece, which was full of tea-caddies and ships in bottles. The collie dog lolled and panted on the flagstones.

'And tell me,' said Peter, 'what way you aren't at school?'

'I got sent home,' I said, 'for not learning the lesson.'

'You must learn your lessons,' said Sophie, setting the fern straight in the tiny window. 'Think what way you'll be in thirty years' time if you don't, a poor ignorant fellow breaking stones in the quarry.'

I took a deep gulp of ale, till my teeth and tongue and palate were awash in a dark seething wave.

'And tell me,' said Peter, 'what will you be when you're big?'

'A sailor,' I said.

'If that wasn't a splendid answer!' cried Peter. 'A sailor. Think of that.'

'My grandfather was a gunner on the *Victory*,' said Sophie. 'He was at Trafalgar. He came home with a wooden leg.'

'That was great days at sea,' said Peter. 'Do you know the ballad of Andrew Ross?'

'No,' I said.

A hen, shaped like a galleon, entered from the road outside. She dipped and swayed round the sleeping dog, and went out again into the sunlight.

'Woman,' said Peter, 'get the squeeze-box.'

Sophie brought a black dumpy cylinder from under the bed, and blew a spurt of dust from it. Peter opened the box and took out a melodeon.

'Listen,' he said. A few preliminary notes as sharp as spray scattered out of the instrument. Then he cleared his throat and began to sing:

> *Andrew Ross an Orkney sailor*
> *Whose sufferings now I will explain*
> *While on a voyage to Barbados,*
> *On board the good ship* Martha Jane.

'That was the name of the ship,' said Sophie, 'the *Martha Jane*.'

'Shut up,' said Peter.

> *The mates and captain daily flogged him*
> *With whips and ropes, I tell you true,*
> *Then on his mangled bleeding body*
> *Water mixed with salt they threw.*

'That's what they used to do in the old days, the black-guards,' said Sophie. 'They would beat the naked backs of the sailors till they were as red as seaweed.'

'Damn it,' said Peter, 'is it you that's reciting this ballad, or is it me?'

> *The captain ordered him to swallow*
> *A thing whereof I shall not name.*
> *The sailors all grew sick with horror*
> *On board the good ship* Martha Jane.

'What was it Andrew Ross had to swallow?' I asked.

'It was too terrible to put in the song,' said Sophie.

'I'll tell you what it was,' said Peter, glaring at me. 'It was *his own dung.*'

The sickness began to work like a yeast in the region of my throat. I took a big swallow of ale to drown it.

Peter sang:

> *When nearly dead they did release him,*
> *And on the deck they did him fling.*
> *In the midst of his pain and suffering*
> *'Let us be joyful,' Ross did sing.*

'He was religious,' said Sophie, 'and the captain was an atheist. That's the way they bad-used him.'

> *The captain swore he'd make him sorry,*
> *And jagged him with an iron bar.*
> *Was not that a cruel treatment*
> *For an honoured British tar!*

The house took a long dizzy lurch to starboard, then slowly righted itself. My knuckles grew white on the edge of the chair. The good ship Myers burrowed again into the fluid hill.

'Mercy,' said Sophie, 'I doubt the boy's too young for a coarse ballad like that.'

> *Justice soon did overtake them*
> *When into Liverpool they came.*
> *They were found guilty of the murder*
> *Committed on the briny main.*

'High time too,' said Sophie. 'The vagabonds!'

> *Soon the fateful hour arrived*
> *That Captain Rogers had to die,*
> *To satisfy offended justice*
> *And hang on yonder gallows high.*

I stood erect on the heaving flagstones. 'Going be sick,' I said.

'The pail!' cried Sophie, 'where's the pail?'

But she was too late. Three strong convulsions went through me, and I spouted thrice. The flagstones were awash. The dog barked. Then the cottage slowly settled on an even keel, and I was sitting in the straw chair, my eyes wet with shame and distress. Not even Andrew Ross's sorrow was like unto my sorrow.

Old Sophie was on her knees with a wet clout and a bucket.

Peter patted me on the shoulder. 'Don't you worry,' he said. 'You're not the first sailor that's been sick on his maiden voyage.'

III

Below the kirkyard the waves stretched long blue necks shoreward. Their manes hissed in the wind, the broken thunder of their hooves volleyed along the beach and echoed far inland among cornfields and peat bogs and trout lochs, and even as far as the quiet group of standing stones at the centre of the island.

I made my way shoreward, walking painfully along a floor of round pebbles. One had to be careful; Isaac of Garth, going home drunk and singing on Saturday nights, was in the habit of smashing his empty bottles on these rocks. He had done it for so many years that the amphitheatre of pebbles above the sand was dense with broken glass – the older fragments worn by the sea to blunt opaque pebbles, the newer ones winking dangerously in the sun. If one of the sharp pieces scored your foot, you might easily bleed to death.

There was no one in sight along the wide curve of the beach, or on the road above. In the kirkyard the grave-digger was up to the hips in a grave he was making for Moll Anderson, who had died at the week-end.

Quickly and cautiously, under a red rock, I took off my clothes – first the grey jersey with the glass button at the neck, next the trousers made out of an old pair of my father's, and finally the blue shirt. Then I ran down to the sea and fell through an incoming wave. Its slow cold hammer drove the air out of my lungs. I thrashed through the water to a rock thirty yards out and clung to it, gasping and shivering. 'Lord,' I thought, 'suppose Miss Ingsetter or my father saw me now!' A shred of cloud raced across the sun, and the world plunged in and out of gloom in a second. And then, for an hour, I was lost in the cry and tumult of the waves. Shags, dark arrows, soared past my plunging face. Gulls cut gleaming arcs and circles against the sky, and traversed long corridors of intense sound. Seals bobbed up and down like bottles in the Sound, and grew still every now and then when I whistled. For a brief eternity I was lost in the cry, the tumult, the salt cleansing ritual of the sea.

The grave-digger paused in his work and, shading his eyes beachward, saw me stumbling out of the waves. He shook his fist at my nakedness. The sand was as hot as new pancakes under my feet. I ran wild and shouting up the beach and fell gasping on my heap of clothes. I lay there for a long time. From very far away, on the other side of the hill, a dog barked. The rockpool shimmered in the heat. The music of the grave-digger's spade rang bright and fragile across the field. Suddenly three words drifted

from the rock above me: 'You naked boy.' I looked up into
the face of Sarah, Abraham the tinker's daughter. She
rarely came to school, but whenever she did she sat like a
wild creature under the map of Canada. She was sprawling
now on the rock with her legs dangling over. Her bare
arms and her thighs, through the red torn dress she wore,
were as brown as an Indian's.

Sarah said, 'I come here every day to watch the boats
passing. When the sun goes down tonight we're moving to
the other end of the island. There's nothing there but the
hill and the hawk over it. Abraham has the lust for rabbits
on him.'

The tinkers have curious voices – angular outcast
flashing accents like the cries of seagulls.

She jumped down from the rock and crouched in front
of me. I had never seen her face so close. Her hair lay
about it in two blue-black whorls, like mussel shells. Her
eyes were as restless as tadpoles, and her small nose shone
as if it had been oiled.

'Sarah,' I said, 'you haven't been to school all week.'

'May God keep me from that place forever,' she said.

With quick curious fingers she began to pick bits of
seaweed out of my hair.

'What will you do,' she said, 'when you're a tall man?
You won't live long, I can tell that. You'll never wear a
gold chain across your belly. You're white like a mush-
room.' She laid two dirty fingers against my shoulder.

'I'm going to be a sailor,' I said, 'or maybe an explorer.'

She shook her head slowly. 'You couldn't sleep with ice
in your hair,' she said.

'I'll take to the roads with a pack then,' I said, 'for I swear to God I don't want to be a minister or a doctor. I'll be a tinker like you.'

She shook her head again. 'Your feet would get broken, tramping the roads we go,' she said.

Her red dress fell open at the shoulder where the button had come out of it. Her shoulder shone in the wind as if it had been rubbed with sweet oils.

She stretched herself like an animal and lay down on the sand with her eyes closed.

I turned away from her and traced slow triangles and circles in the sand. I turned a grey stone over; a hundred forky-tails seethed from under it like thoughts out of an evil mind. From across the field came the last chink of the grave-digger's spade – the grave was dug now; the spade leaned, miry and glittering, against the kirkyard wall. Two butterflies, red and white over the rockpool, circled each other in silent ecstasy, borne on the stream of air. They touched for a second, then fell apart, flickering in the wind, and the tall grass hid them. I turned quickly and whispered in Sarah's ear.

Her first blow took me full in the mouth. She struck me again on the throat as I tried to get to my feet. Then her long nails were in my shoulder and her wild hair fell across my face. She thrust me back until my shoulder-blades were in the burning sand and my eyes wincing in the full glare of the sun. She dug sharp knees into my ribs until I screamed. Then she ravelled her fingers through my hair and beat my head thrice on the hard sand. Through my shut lids the sun was a big shaking gout of blood.

At last she let me go. 'Next time I come to the school,' she said, looking down at me with dark smiling eyes, 'I'll sit at your desk, under the yellow head of the poet.' She bent over quickly and held her mouth against my throat for as long as it takes a wave to gather and break. Her hair smelt of ditch-water and grass fires. Then she was gone.

I put on the rest of my clothes, muttering through stiff lips, 'You bitch! O you bloody bully, I'll have the attendance officer after you in ten minutes, just see if I don't!'

As I left the beach, walking slowly, I could see her swimming far out in the Sound.

She waved and shouted, but I turned my face obstinately towards the white road that wound between the kirkyard and the cornfield. The salt taste of blood was in my mouth.

IV

The grave-digger had finished making Moll Anderson's grave. He was sitting on the shaft of his barrow, smoking a clay pipe. As I turned in at the gate he wagged his beard at me, for he did not associate this shy decently clad boy with the naked insolence he had seen running out of the sea half an hour before. I wandered away from him among the branching avenues of tomb-stones – the tall urns and frozen angels of modern times; the fiery pillars with the names of grandfathers on them; the scythe-and-hourglass slates of the eighteenth century; and the lichened leprous tombs of a still earlier age. This small field was honeycombed with the dead of generations – farmers with stony faces; young girls rose-cheeked with consumption; infants who had sighed once or twice and turned back to the darkness; stern Greek-loving ministers; spinsters with nipped breasts and pursed mouths. I stood on the path, terrified for a moment at the starkness and universality of shrouds; at the infinite dead of the island, their heads pointing westward in a dense shoal, adrift on the slow tide that sets towards eternity.

My dreaming feet brought me to a low tombstone set in the east wall:

HERE LIES BURIED

A FOREIGN SEAMAN,

OF UNKNOWN NAME AND NATIONALITY

WHOM THE SEA CAST UP ON THIS ISLAND,

JUNE THE SIXTH, 1856

*'Though I take the wings of
the morning, and flee to the
uttermost places of the sea.'*

I closed my eyes and saw a little Basque town between the bay and the mountains.

The feast of Our Lady of the Sea was over. The nets and the oars had been blessed. The candles were still burning in their niches among the rocks.

Now the young people are dancing in a square that lies white and black under the moon.

The musician slouches, as if he were drunk or half asleep, against the fountain. Only his hand is alive, hovering over the strings like a vibrant bird.

The young people are dancing now in long straight lines. The partners clap their hands and bow to each other. They shout; the dark faces are lit up with a flash of teeth. They move round each other with momentarily linked arms. They incline towards each other, their hands on their knees, and stamp their feet. It is all precision, disciplined fluency, a stylized masque of coupling.

Older men and women sit gossiping on the doorsteps. Occasionally they sip from tall glasses. One, a fat man with a yellow beard, looks often through a gap in the houses, at a ship anchored in the harbour.

An old shawled woman stands alone, in the shadow of the church. No one speaks to her; the seal of separation is on her. She is the guardian of the gates of birth and death. In this village she comes to deliver every wailing child, she goes to shroud every quiet corpse. Her eyes are in the dust, from which all this vanity has come, and to which it must return.

The hand over the guitar moves into a new swirling rhythm. Now the square is all one coloured wheel, a great wavering orange blossom.

Suddenly there is an interruption. A tall bearded sailor appears at an alley-opening and walks slowly across the square. The guitar falters. The dance is frozen. The old dark woman raises her head. The officer points to one of the dancers and crooks his finger: he must come, immediately, the ship is sailing tonight.

The seaman – he is only a boy – turns once and looks back. A girl has raised her apron to her face. The yellow-bearded man rises from his doorstep and makes a gesture of blessing: 'Lady of Waters, guard him this day and all days till the sail returns to the headland.'

Above the village a cross stands among the stars. Through a long silence comes the sound of the sea. The last votive candle gutters and goes out among the rocks.

The little town of moonlight and music will never see that sail again. Her voyage has ended on a northern rock. All her sailors have vanished down the path of gull and lobster, scattered in a wild Atlantic storm. One broken shape only was lifted out of the seaweed. Curious hands have carried the nameless thing in procession across the fields. They have clipped the rags from it and combed its hair, and covered the crab-eaten face. And though there was no priest to sing Latin over it, a Calvinist minister said, 'All flesh is grass, and the glory of flesh is as the flower thereof' – the orange blossom of Spain and the little blue Orkney primula, whose circles of beauty are full and radiant for a short time only; and then, drifting winterward, or broken with June tempest, lay separate shining arcs in the dust . . .

My slow circuitous walk had brought me to the new gaping hole in the earth. The grave-digger was still sitting on his barrow. He bored a sidelong glance into me and said: 'There's only one way of coming into the world, but ah, God, there's two or three ways of going out.'

'That's a fact,' I said.

'Would you like,' he said, 'to see what a man *truly* is?'

Not understanding, I gave a quick nod. He groped with his hand into the small hill of clay beside the open grave, and brought out a skull. Carefully he wiped it on his moleskin trousers. 'That's you,' he said, 'and me, and the laird, and Frank the idiot. Just that.'

He laughed. 'There's nothing here to make your face so white. It's as harmless as can be, this bone. It's at peace, and not before time. When it lived it had little rest, with its randy eyes and clattering tongue. This skull belonged to Billy Anderson, Moll's grandfather. He was twice in jail and fathered three illegitimate bairns. O, he was a thieving, drunken, fighting character, and it was a good day for him when we threw him in here. Wasn't it, Billy?' he said to the skull, blowing smoke into its eye-hollows. 'Wasn't it, boy?' . . . The skull grinned back at him.

From the other side of the loch the school bell rang the dismissal.

Over the hill from the village, like a procession of beetles, came the mourners.

V

After I had finished my lessons that evening, I was summoned into the shop.

My father was sitting at the counter between a barrel of paraffin oil and a great dark coil of tobacco. There was a jar of sweets at his elbow. Over his head hung jerseys and scarves and stockings, with price tickets on them. The lamp swung from the hook in the ceiling, smoking a little. There was always a good smell in the shop.

'It's thee, John,' he said, raising his head from the ledger for a moment. 'Sit down, boy.' He counted the sticks of toffee in a glass jar and then said, 'How did thu get on at the school today?'

'Fine,' I said.

'I've been thinking about thee,' he said, 'what to make o' thee, once thee school-days are over.'

He gathered up a handful of coins, and rang them one by one back into the till. Then he marked the ledger on his desk with a pencil.

'There's no future in this shop, I can tell thee that,' he said. 'The profits are getting smaller every year. The reason is, the folk are leaving the island. They're going to the cities and the colonies. Not a month passes but another family leaves.

'And then they send to the mail-order places in the south for their clothes and their ironmongery. A great lot of them do that. They forget that we depend on each other for our livelihood in a small island like this.

'And there's debts too,' he said. 'For instance, Mistress Anderson who was buried this afternoon died owing more than six pounds. So it'll be a poor inheritance for thee, this shop,' he said.

He licked his pencil and wrote more figures in the ledger. His hair glittered frailly in the lamp-light.

'I had a word with Miss Ingsetter this afternoon about thee,' he went on. 'She called at the shop after school for some fly-papers. She seemed surprised thu weren't home yet . . . I made a point of asking her about thee. She says thu're an able boy, good beyond the general run at reading and writing and history. Not so bright at the mathematics. Sometimes thu're inclined to be inattentive

and dreamy, she says. At times, only at times. But there's
no harm in the boy, she said, and he's by no means
stupid. And it's my opinion, she said, he ought to go to
the grammar school in Kirkwall for a secondary education, once he turns twelve.'

'I want to be a sailor,' I said.

'The dreaminess,' he said, 'you take from your mother
. . . After the school comes the university. That'll cost
money, a power of money. Still, I'm not barehanded, I
haven't neglected to provide for things like that. With a
degree in thee pocket, thu could enter *the professions*.
Think of that.'

'It's the sea I have a hankering for,' I said. 'Uncle Ben
said he could get me into the Saint Line, any time I
wanted.'

'The ministry is an honourable profession,' he said.
'There isn't a lot of money in it, but you get a free
manse, and I can tell you old MacFarland doesn't spend
a fortune on food. He gets a hen here and a pound of
butter there and a sack of tatties from the other place.
On his rounds, you understand, his visitations. Cheese at
the Bu, and fish from Quoys, and a fleece for spinning
from Westburn, all for nothing. And nobody can say the
work is strenuous.'

'Supper is ready,' my mother sang out from the kitchen.

'Now doctoring is strenuous, there's no doubt about
that. They haven't a moment to call their own. They
can't even be sure of a night's sleep. There's always
somebody thundering at Doctor Leslie's door after midnight with the toothache, or a pain in the guts, or a

hook's got stuck in their hand. It's no wonder he's taken to the drink lately. But, putting all that aside, medicine is a fine calling. Plenty of money in it too, if you can get them to pay their bills.'

'I spoke to Mother,' I said. 'She would like fine for me to be a deep-sea captain. She's going to write to Ben.'

'The law,' he said, 'is a different thing. Not that there's anything wrong with it, if you understand, but there's a shady side to it, there's a certain amount of trickery about it that makes the ordinary honest man wonder sometimes. You can hardly open a newspaper without seeing some lawyer or other in trouble for embezzling his client's money, and carrying on. You'll hear a couple of them arguing a case like mad in the courts, and then, half an hour later, there they'll be walking down the street together cheek by jowl . . . John,' he said, 'never go to law if you can possibly help it. Not but what there aren't honest lawyers too.'

He unscrewed the lid from a bottle of black-striped balls. He took out a couple between his fingers and handed them across the counter.

'If there's one place I have a longing to see,' I said, 'it's Japan.'

He suddenly withdrew his hand and dropped the black-striped balls back into the jar.

'Not before your food,' he said, licking his fingers. 'I forgot . . . Then there's teaching—'

'Are you coming for your supper,' chanted my mother impatiently, 'or are you not?'

Outside the dog began to bark. There was a clattering of hooves and wheels over the cobbles. The poultry squawked like mad in the yard. 'Mercy,' said my father, running to the door, 'it's the tinkers. *The hens!*'

I followed him out, into the moonlight. The tinker's cart was opposite the door now. Abraham sat on the shaft. He cracked his whip and cried to the grey pony. In the cart sat Mary his wife with an infant slung behind her in a tartan shawl. Sarah walked alongside with her arms full of wild lupins.

They were going to the other end of the island where the rabbits were thick, to camp there.

'Giddap!' cried Abraham and cracked his whip. 'That's a fine dog you have there, Mister Sigurdson,' he shouted to my father. 'I'll take a half-pound of bogey roll, and I'll pay you when I come back along next week.'

'No,' said my father sternly, 'you'll pay now, for you owe me sixteen and six already.'

'Hello, Sarah,' I said. She stood on the road and looked at me through the dark blue congregated spires of lupins.

'Are you seeking a tin pail, mistress?' yelled Abraham to my mother, who had come out and was standing at the corner of the house guarding the hens.

'Yes,' she said, 'I'll need one when you come back by next week.'

Suddenly my father was furious. 'We need no tin pails!' he shouted. 'There's plenty of tin pails in the shop!'

'Next week-end, mistress,' cried Abraham. He stood between the shafts and cracked his whip. 'Giddap!' he yelled. The wheels rolled in crazy circles over the cobbles and stars streamed from the pony's hooves. There was a sudden wild *cluck-cluck-clucking* from inside the cart as it moved off. Sarah stood looking at us, smiling through her screen of lupins.

My father went back into the shop, muttering. My mother stood at the corner of the house and watched them out of sight. 'One of the hens is missing,' she said. 'I darena tell thee father. He would have the police at them for sure.'

A wave of purple blossom rose in front of the moon and showered over me.

Soon the racket died away at the far end of the village. Sarah's mockery sounded from a distance of three fields. I turned back into the house. My face was wet with dew and petals, and the moon raged above the mission hall wilder than ever.

'The very idea!' cried my father from inside the shop. 'A sailor! A tin pail! *The thieves!*'

Time was skulls and butterflies and guitars.

The Three Islands

It was a bad day for fishing. We should not have agreed to go out with him at all. But Sander's creels had lain there in the torn firth for a week. Some of them would have been smashed over the week-end. Sander said he would give Bill and me two pounds each to help him that morning.

We left the beach as soon as it was light. Cold lumps of sea met us in the Sound. Sander said some of his creels were off Eynhallow. 'What kind of a place is that to set creels?' said Bill in a low voice, so that Sander couldn't hear.

The sea was going in a spate between Rousay and Eynhallow, broken and white as if it poured over different levels. This was The Roost. The *Emily* took a lot of water. It was still an hour till the tide turned. We got in under the lee of the island and began hauling. Only two creels were broken. There was a lobster in all the others and two lobsters in three of them. We baited the creels and set them again.

'A good place,' said Sander.

Eynhallow lay like a green foundered ship in the middle of The Roost. The walls of the small medieval monastery were still standing. 'For God's sake,' said Bill, 'what way would monks have passed all their lives in a place like that?'

'They would have fished,' said Sander, 'the same as we're doing. And they might have kept a pig or two.' . . . He drew up another creel – a lobster clashed its blue armour at us.

'I expect they prayed a lot,' said Bill.

They had all gone to the haddocks. They left Andrew behind, a young brother from Scotland, to feed the pigs and keep the fires going. He sat in the deep west window of the chapel that summer morning with a feather, an ink-pot, and a bit of old parchment. The animals were fed, the fire was banked, the light was burning in the sanctuary. He wrote: 'What may I scrieve but anerlie the tale of Everyman, an erst puissant earl that goeth now in beggar's rags? Everyman I am, unkent I gang thorough this usurpit kingrik. Meikle men I erst had governaunce of. They are turned from me, ilk ane. Ride they now, proud horsemen, thorough corn and pasture, their names are callit Lust, Greed, Gluttony, Sloth, Pride, Envy, Anger, meikle up-starts, meikle anarchy. I sit at the corner of the stye, a gangrel swineherd, that once held all that fair land in feif for a great king. And what if he should come suddenly again and seek of me a reckoning? Hard it would go then with this swineherd. Ilk hour my sharp thoughts seek to slander and to slay the king I hae been traitor til. *Whatna king?* they sneer. *We have kent no sic king. That king is thrust forth in banishment eterne. This is but an imagined king. The king is deid.* Yea, but did I not break his bread one time? Bear I not yet among thae rags the most precious cup of his passion? I will yet keep that from the mouth of beasts. Wherefore I say, even among these ruts and stinks and rootings, whereof I am fallen lord, *Adveniat regnum tuum.*'

The scribe dips his feather in the stone jar of ink and writes the fable slowly on the skin. Each word takes a long time to shape. But there is no hurry. He is anxious over the curve and fall of every letter, how it leans to the horizontal like a ship balanced and freighted. It carries a cargo from eternity into time, an allegory, a God-tiding. Maybe an Eynhallow monk will read it after he is dust. He forms another letter with care and reverence. He dips his feather once more in the stone ink-well; then quickly raises his head. He has heard the scrape of a boat on the beach.

*

'I set a score of creels behind Gairsay too,' said Sander. He swung the tiller round.

It was much quieter in the middle of the firth. Eynhallow fell away behind us, a ghost in the rain. Clouds and sea were all mixed up in one dreich swirl. We took plenty of water from both. It was raining hard most of the time. The sea was grey. The sky was grey too, shading to black over Eday but bright like scraped lead over Gairsay and Rendall.

'Here we are,' said Bill. The floats rocked on the swell.

We had a worse haul off Gairsay. Every second creel was empty. But there was none broken. It was more sheltered working, except for the rain that kept coming in squalls.

'Bastard rain,' said Bill, squeezing it out of his beard.

'You boys swear too much,' said Sander, who was a Plymouth Brother. 'The rain is good rain, for the Lord gives it.'

Gairsay rose out of the firth, a steep hill, with one large empty farm. We baited the creels again and set them in new water.

'That's a poor lonely place,' said Bill, 'with only sheep on it, and yet it seems to have been well farmed once. Look at that big steading.'

'That's Langskaill,' said Sander.

Sander swung in a creel with two lobsters in it. One of them was dead. The lobsters had jousted like knights at the sea bottom, in their tarry arena. Sander pulled out the live one and tied his victorious claws with twine.

'A poor island,' said Bill.

In the long hall of Gairsay sat a man with an alehorn at his elbow and a crude map of broken western coasts on his knee. The spring sowing was over. The ship *Drake* was out of the shed. The women had put on board the ale and the new bread and the salted meat. Ploughmen and shepherds carried into her sails and swords and oars – until harvest summoned them home they would be seamen, Vikings. Towns and churches would know of them. *A furore Normanorum, libera nos, Domine.* The last roller was taken from under the keel. The man folded his map and stood up. Beside the barn a girl covered her face in her apron. Sweyn Asleifson the captain was on board now. The anchor was raised. The ship was on the sea.

Summer came, with tall skies and surges of wind in the green corn. Gairsay was full of the voices of women, birds, children – sometimes a quiet harp on either side of the small twilight, for Sweyn's poet had stayed at home this summer.

It is August now, the last days of the hot month. The girl with the milkpail sees a square sail between Rousay and Evie. Is it the *Drake?* No, this ship has a heavy crimson sail, like a cloud after sunset. She sits on the water like the *Drake,* it's true. She leans between wind and sea like the *Drake.* She fits the horizon like the *Drake.* The girl drops her pail and runs into Langskaill. And soon the light dancer, the masker with the crimson sail, is anchored off the rock. It is the *Drake.*

What has the ship brought back to Orkney? Sweyn Asleifson the Viking captain, Rolf, Grettir, Thorkeld, Thorvald, Thorfinn, Arn, Einar, Erling, Bui, Jon, Eylot. But where are Hrut the ploughman and Rollo the shepherd?

Listen first to the story of Hrut.

Hrut grazed his foot on a broken shell at Uist, on the beach, on his way up to an alehouse there. After his hangover the next day a worse trouble came on him. The graze began to beat and throb, and all his leg swole and turned blue, and soon after the thunder reached his groin Hrut was dead. Not much attention was paid to the death of Hrut; he was an unpopular man. And Rollo? Ah, that was different, there was nothing undignified or comical about the end of Rollo.

Listen now to the story of Rollo.

There was a strong fortified house in Penzance and the Orkneymen were round it for two days with axes and fire and loud weighted insults. But the place was well and skilfully defended. Those inside had no lack of arrows, stones, buckets of boiling tar. The Orkneymen could not get near the place because of concentrated fire from the slotted windows above and on each side of the main door. Rollo said, 'Somebody must get to that door and hack it down.' So he walked up to the door with his axe in his hand. A deluge of tar spattered and smoked at his heel. An arrow went clean through his beard and stuck quivering in the ground. A large stone glanced off his helmet with a sound like a church bell. 'I will perhaps have a headache in the morning,' said Rollo. He reached the door and was in the act of raising his axe to demolish the lock when three arrows struck him simultaneously. The arrow ends stuck out of his back like rapturous birds. 'Now I don't need to worry about that headache in the morning,' said Rollo. His axe clattered on the stones and he fell dead in front of the house. The Orkneymen besieged the house all night but they couldn't get in. They set fire to the barns and stables and sailed for Scilly at first light next morning. Everyone agreed that Rollo had had a good death.

What had the *Drake* brought back to Gairsay?

An Irish girl in a long yellow dress.

And also?

Twelve large golden coins and three hundred and forty-one silver coins, a barrel of red wine, bulbs of lilies and daffodils from Scilly, a tapestry of Greek gods with a sword slash in it (but Thora will mend it with her coloured wools), two English hounds (a third died of sea-sickness in the Minch), a spinning wheel from the Hebrides, a church bell and a silver chalice from Iona (which will be returned next year, Sweyn having expressly forbidden the looting of churches in compliance with a request from his friend William, Bishop of Orkney, and having punished the thief Thorvald by keeping him at the oar and depriving him of ale for three nights and days), seven talking birds in a cage, a great web of crimson broadcloth which they had sewn on to their sails so that the *Drake* might have a stylish homecoming.

And what did they bring?

The death of a Summer.

The fields were as yellow now as the Irish girl's dress. They walked between the yellow fields and the long hall. Inside, the sound of a solitary harp. The poet had stayed at home all summer, among the women and the birds and the growing corn. He would put the story of that voyage in verse later, in winter, over the fires, so that even the sailors themselves would relish the poem better than the voyage, and glimpse a beauty behind the boasting and the brutality.

*

'And I have a score of creels at the tail of Egilsay,' said Sander. 'I would like to get them hauled too. That's the lot then.'

The wind had freshened a bit and it was driving the rain northwards, over Eday and Westray. The dark curtains trailed farther from us. The clouds brightened and here and there let through some sun. Away to the left Eynhallow was momentarily transfigured, then the flying bronze touched the cliffs of Rousay and moved on over the Rousay hills, Kearfea and Blotchnifiold.

We were taking plenty of sea though.

Sander pushed the tiller from him. The *Emily* went round in a wide circle. We ran into sudden pools of sun; the sea lost its greyness; it flashed with changing colour like the heart of an opal; then it was grey again; and the round-towered stone kirk of Egilsay took for a moment the uncertain glory.

We pulled the creels in quickly, with stiff hands. It was a

middling catch, twelve lobsters from the score of creels. We baited the creels again and set them a little to the west.

'And when we get back,' said Bill, 'I'm going to sit a whole hour at the pub fire and I'm going to drink three double whiskies straight off, one after the other.'

'You boys drink too much,' said Sander mildly.

'No water in the glass,' said Bill. 'Between rain and sea I've tholed enough water for one day. And tonight,' he said, looking at Sander defiantly, 'I'm going to the women.'

The sky was clearing quickly. The fading rain was a dark bruise in the north. Surge after surge of light went over the firth and the islands, until Egilsay, the island of Saint Magnus the Martyr, stood at last in full hard light.

'Goodbye, Egilsay,' said Bill. 'What a place! We didn't get much out of you.'

Sander turned the *Emily* round.

The church island, Egilsay, beaten on by three lights – sea, sky, sanctity.

What had Egilsay done to deserve holiness?

Nothing.

It was a poor island, bog and rock, not beautiful, though there were beautiful islands lying all round it. Then the axe and the skull held their dialogue over a new furrow.

The bishop would not have sent one of his best priests there – I think perhaps an old man, a bit cross with sciatica and boredom. Would his face light up when he saw a child or a new lamb or a daffodil? Perhaps the old withered apples of his face shone a little then.

One April morning there was a strange face among the peasant women kneeling at Mass. The man had good clothes and his head and beard were barbered. The old priest had never seen him before. *Introibo ad altare Dei.* He went up the three steps of the altar. Then, as always, he wove his mortal thoughts into the heavy golden warp of the Mass.

'Now to God and the saints and my people and this stranger I confess that I have sinned. They in their turn confess to God and the saints and to me that they too have sinned. The hand knocks the breast in contrition.

'The water and the wine are on the stone ledge. The boy guards them. Outside, at the door, there is the clang of a plough or a sword. The world goes about its business.

Dominus vobiscum.

'They return me the same fair greeting.

'The Epistle. The boy carries the Word, circling round, dipping and fluttering like a bird, between one horn of the altar and the other. *Cleanse my lips.* They stand, the women of Egilsay. The blessed Gospel assures them that Christ is risen from the dead. It is the morning of Easter Monday. A man risen out of his grave. Can they believe that? They believe it, they are poor ignorant passionate women. The cultured stranger in his broadcloth might have more difficulty in swallowing such a thing.

'Metal against stone, outside. Loud voices. There are more strangers in Egilsay today than just this one stranger inside the church. Probably there is to be a hunt. The lairds have come from all over Orkney with hawks and nets and dogs.

Credo in unum Deum.

'The boy comes eagerly to me with the wine and the water. He it is who, like the boy with the loaves and fishes, brings the gifts of all here present to the Lord. Little enough they have to offer, those people. A few blades of corn, a few crabs and sillocks. They are exceedingly poor, and the war of the earls has made them poorer than ever. Horsemen in the corn, Vikings among the nets. This bread and this wine is the sign of their giving. With these they offer God everything that is theirs – their bunions, their jars of oil, bright hearth-stones, the long nights they lie awake listening to the sea on the rock when the fishermen are out. What the stranger could offer I do not know. He looks like a man of no small possessions, of whom we are told that it will be difficult for them to enter the Kingdom. We cannot tell. Priest and people, we offer together the bread and wine, our sacrifice.

Orate, fratres

'Saint and angel and holy soul are summoned to witness the things we do. A whole heaven of shining ones is crowded into this stone kirk, as thick as corn on the side of Kearfea on a bright windy August day. Will it be, perhaps, that one or two of those same earthy people will be quickened, that the green shoot and the golden stalk will soar out of their brutishness, fit ones for the threshing-floors of purgatory? Doubtless. All of them, I pray. For this we were born.

'The little cry of the altar bell is lost in the clash of swords outside.

'Once more I have done it. What seems to be impossible has happened. The Body and the Blood of Our Lord lie on the altar before me. It is accomplished. The church is drowned in a terrible and beautiful silence.

'A mouse scrapes and scrapes in the hollow wall of the church.

Agnus Dei qui tollis peccata mundi miserere nobis.

'God is come among us. Our little gifts of bread and wine He returns to us loaded with blessing and beauty and peace and love and glory illimitable. *Ecce Agnus Dei.* Himself he gives to us. I show them the Lord. I place the Host on the few rough tongues and one smooth tongue. The stranger also has received communion.

Corpus Domini nostri Jesu Christi custodiat animam tuam in vitam aeternam.

'And the stranger whose face is all an agony of fear and resolution goes back to his place among the peasants who suffer after another fashion.

Ite, missa est.

'The swords outside are louder now, the voices rise into a chant: "Magnus, Magnus, come out, Magnus."

'It is for this stranger, Magnus, that there is all this clash and outcry in Egilsay today. I am sending him out among those swords, into an anger of which I know nothing. I make a quick silent prayer for him, rinsing the chalice with fresh wine.

'And so now when I bless the people of Egilsay at the end of the Mass, I bless him in particular whose face is as bright and as doomed as a stone with spring sunlight on it that the builders will soon gather into a new wall. *Benedicat vos omnipotens Deus, Pater et Filius et Spiritus Sanctus.*'

*

We landed three boxes of lobsters from the flattie. Sander took his purse out of his hip pocket and carefully thumbed out four pounds, two pounds to Bill and two pounds to me. Then he crossed the field to the licensed grocer's to phone to the Fishermen's Society.

Bill and I hauled the flattie high up till its bow was cleaving the clover and buttercups of the links, out of reach of the long waves.

Sander came back from the licensed grocer's with a half-bottle of whisky in his hand. He uncorked it ceremonially. We squatted on the pier in our shiny oilskins, in the lee of the boat shed. The lobsters shuffled slowly in their boxes. Sander gave the half-bottle to Bill first. Bill held it up and said, 'Skol.' He pushed it into his mouth and tilted it. A little runnel of whisky ran down his chin. He grunted as if he had been hit in the stomach. He wiped the top of the half-bottle with his sleeve and passed it to me. I drank from it and passed it to Sander. The spirit licked round my cold guts like flame.

'No,' said Sander piously. 'I have never drunk spirits or ale in my life.' He gave the half-bottle to Bill again.

'You don't know what you're missing,' said Bill.

'I'm very beholden to you boys for coming out with me on a morning like this,' said Sander.

Bill handed the half-bottle to me. I had another drink and then said, 'But you paid us well.'

Nothing more was said till the whisky was all drunk and Bill sent the empty half-bottle crashing among the stones of the beach.

Then Sander said, 'You hauled the flattie too high up. It was ebbing when we landed.'

The Seller of Silk Shirts

I crossed yesterday to the island of Quoylay to sell silk shirts to the people. I am a Sikh boy. My name over here is Johnny.

First was the boatman. He says to another man in the stern, in a voice that goes up and down like singing:

> 'Do what you like, says I,
> But when in future
> You want a loan of two pounds,
> Don't come, says I, to my door,
> Inga,
> After what you said and did in the village
>   on Saturday night.'

At the croft above the pier a man was building a new pig-sty. He was carrying stones from the beach. A boy was carrying stones from the beach. A girl also was carrying stones from the beach. The girl stopped and made tea . . . Those pigs have the expectation of living in a beautiful little house made of stones that have been under the sea.

There is a house where is a telephone and also a shop. Going to such a place I have made a mistake, they also sell shirts though coarse of cotton and wool, not silk shirts. This is strange, also they sell tobacco, sugar, rope, many things. The lady there was most fat and most kind.

I have gone then to a house on a hill. Many hens promenade at the door. I have much fear of the dog but there are words in the inside darkness that say, '*Down, Laddie, down.*' What an old lady dusts the chair for my backside to sit! What an old man of words! His wrists were ornamented with blue anchors. Their ale was such that I might have fallen asleep on the chair. I have sold a silk scarf to the lady, that she will wear to the agricultural show next week, I am thinking.

Now did the next big house prove to be the minister's house. There are many unused rooms, none but the minister and his woman, what shame, a hundred of my people might live and sleep there. He has made remarks about bathing in the holy River Ganges that show signal knowledge. No refreshment, neither tea nor ale nor cigarettes, though I have complimented him on the immense number and blackness of his books.

Here is a beautiful girl living alone in a place with broken windows beside the loch. I make myself delightful to this girl. There is no dog. There is no old person behind the door angry. Instead there is a new round cake smoking on the table. This girl says, 'Lucky you have come today. At the week-end I had no money, my national assistance was spent. On Saturday night by hard means I got money in the village. Lucky you have come, I must buy a birthday present for Tom the boatman, a silk shirt would be beautiful.'

Yet she has not enough money for a silk shirt. Yet I have sold her one cheap, a bargain, a yellow silk shirt spread out wide like a sleeping butterfly on the little flowered bed she sleeps in.

Such was the beautiful poor girl I sold a shirt to, beside the loch. Her name was called Inga. Even so with the cheapness of the sale I had thirty-five per cent profit. Pretty was Inga.

Three things troubled me crossing the field to the hospitable farm of Greengyres. First, I entered inadvertently my foot into a rabbit hole. Second, I was threatened by a female cow with horns. Third, needing to pass water I was faced wherever I turned by near and distant windows. Yet at the delightful farm of Greengyres were met all my difficulties. There I sold no less than one shirt, four pairs sox, six handkerchiefs, all articles silken.

The schoolmistress was forbidding and in a mood to send me away till I have told her of my graduation from the University of Bombay with B.A. degree and the imminence of my Ph.D. studying at the University of Edinburgh in October on a thesis, 'The Topography of the Mystical Books of William Blake'. She has graduated from that same university. She is not like Inga, pretty. She has long black hairs on her lip, and a wart.

Much walking I did on that island.

On the other side of the hill were three spreading peats, a man and two women, in the sun. Here was much mirth. I say to the man, 'You have no shirt, therefore you must buy one of my silk shirts.' All laid down their implements with laughter. A woman said, 'Nobody wears a silk shirt cutting peats.' We laughed greatly. I then responded with this remark, 'Yet when the peats are cut and brought home, then will come the hour of celebration that will necessitate the wearing of a silk shirt!' There I stayed with merriment for five-and-twenty minutes, drinking tea from a flask and smoking two cigarettes. Truly these were merry peat-cutters.

In the evening at the stipulated hour I returned to the boat. The boatman was saying to another man in the stern, but really with the speech of those islanders it seems like singing:

> 'So then, what could I say?
> For my birthday
> Had she not baked a small cake
> And brought on her arm
> A shirt yellow as buttercups
>   this very afternoon?
> That way
> All our troubles ended.'

In the island of Quoylay I have sold seven shirts, three pairs sox, twenty-one handkerchiefs, five scarves, and to Inga I have given a free headsquare depicting the dance called 'The Shake', though I have told her it was the god Krishna among milkmaidens.

The Wheel

On Saturday night in the fishermen's pub there's always plenty of noise and smoke. By nine o'clock you can hardly see the bottles at the far end of the bar for reek, and you have to shout to make yourself heard by the man at your elbow. There's darts and arguments and dominoes and stories going on all round, and the erratic jingling commerce of silver and glass across the bar.

At five past nine, as always, Robert appeared at the door. He said in his coarse throaty voice, 'Have any o' you men seen Walls?'

At once there was silence. The dart thrower held his hand. The drinkers paused in the act of lifting their pints. Old Tom the barman's hand froze on the lever. The whole pub was turned to stone for about one second.

'No,' said old Tom, 'he hasn't been here tonight.'

Robert turned and shambled out through the door.

Immediately the pub resumed its normal life. The dart flew at the board. The pints rose and fell. Money and glasses rang on the counter. The farmers sitting round the table laughed and pressed their knees. Everything went on as before, with perhaps a little more abandon, now that Robert had taken the gorgon's head away.

*

Robert followed the same ritual every Saturday night. His first visit was to the pub. His next call was to the Salvation Army ring at the pierhead.

The band and songsters were rendering 'Count Your Blessings' when Robert arrived. He walked slowly over the cobbles and stood behind Miriam, a girl with big grey eyes and golden hair.

'Has Walls been here tonight?' he whispered to her.

Miriam, still singing, shook her head and smiled gently at Robert. One by one the girl Salvationists shook their heads at him. 'No,' whispered Miriam through the brazen clamour, 'not tonight. But some day soon we'll all be seeing him.'

Robert looked closely at the three men there, as if the face of Walls might be concealed under one of those black brims and blood-and-fire badges, behind one of those shining joyous instruments; for hadn't Walls once joined the Army in a fit of repentance after a drunken spree, and learned to play the cornet before he lapsed again . . . ? But none of those faces belonged to the lost one. Robert turned away slowly.

*

He walked up the street to a narrow two-storey house. There the holy rag-time was no longer audible. He opened the outer door and climbed slowly upstairs. At the top of the house he tapped at a door with a printed notice on it: *H. Leask, Dress-maker.*

'Come in, Robert,' cried a deep voice from inside. Robert tip-toed in and sat down beside the fern.

A huge red-faced woman was seated at a sewing-machine, working on a dress for a young girl, half-finished, covered with alternate roses and swallows. All the time the woman spoke to Robert she went on working.

'What's new in the town tonight?' she said.

'There's nothing new at all,' said Robert, 'except that Harold the shepherd was disgraceful drunk in the pub, and the Army's given Miriam a new red band for her bonnet.'

'Fancy that,' said the woman.

There was a long difficult silence. Then Robert said, slowly and hesitatingly, 'I'm thinking o' turning owre the tattie patch in the morning . . . and I wanted to tell Walls . . . so he could order a load o' dung . . . but he hasna been home . . . and I was wondering . . .' His words trailed off into silence.

'You was wondering what?' said the woman patiently.

'I was wondering . . . the way he's always coming back and fore here . . . maybe . . . if he was, you ken . . . up here beside you?'

She looked at Robert with her black eyes and said, 'No, Robert, I'm sorry to say he hasna been up here at all tonight, or any other night this while back.'

'O well, then I'll be going,' said Robert, getting to his feet.

She stopped work, listening to his clumsy feet going down the stair. She put her hand across her eyes and bent her head over the cloud of cotton, over the crumpled wings and crumpled petals. Her face was blank and streaming.

*

After that, Robert walked up the hill between the fields, to a stone house that looked out over the islands and the burning hills. He walked slowly now, as if he was afraid of something.

Even before he reached the door, as he stood lurching and hesitant on the gravel, it was opened by a neat little man with a beard and a grey polo-neck jersey. 'You'll be wanting to know about Walls,' said the man.

'Yes, captain,' said Robert timidly. 'Maybe you can tell me, for I mind him saying he might be coming to you for a reference, if he decides to go to the whaling next year.'

'I'll tell you,' said the man, 'the same as I've told you every Saturday night for the last two years.'

'No,' said Robert, 'don't tell me that.'

'I will tell you,' said the man, 'for it's the truth, and the sooner you realize it the better.'

'No,' said Robert, 'never mind, I'll go home.'

The old sailor seized him by the arm. 'Listen,' he said, in a loud angry voice. 'Walls is cold and in his grave. Didn't I see him laid out in the mortuary? Didn't I take the head of his coffin when we carried him to the kirkyard? Didn't I put a stone up for him, with his name and his years carved on it?'

Robert shook himself free. He gave the little man one terrified look. Then he turned between the new daffodils and the fuchsia bush on to the road. His feet shuffled and knocked into each other in his haste to be gone.

'You better behave yourself,' yelled the old sailor after him. 'You better not come annoying folk every Saturday night, asking after a dead man! There's places for fools like you! Now I'm warning you!'

*

At home in the little stone house at the edge of the pier, Robert laid the table for two, as he always did, and put on the kettle to boil. He opened a drawer in the dresser and thumbed through a pile of letters and cuttings. At last he found the scrap of newspaper he was looking for. He put on his steel spectacles, and sitting down in the straw-back chair beside the fire read the print on it:

'Last Saturday night a sad discovery was made, when the body of a local sailor William Walls was found at low tide among the rocks under his own pier. Mr Walls, who was fifty years of age, was of a jovial disposition, and will be much missed by his many friends in the locality. The news came as a particular shock to Mr Walls' cronies with whom he had spent a happy evening only a matter of hours before the tragic discovery was made. For some years he sailed in the Swallow Line under Captain Stevens, a distinguished son of the islands. Mr Walls was a bachelor, and lived at the South End with his friend Mr Robert Jansen, with whom sympathy is expressed at this time. The funeral, which was well attended, took place at the local cemetery on Tuesday afternoon, and was conducted by Lieutenant Rogers of the Salvation Army, with which sect the deceased had been connected at one period in his career.

Robert carefully replaced the cutting in the drawer. He put a spoon of sugar and a spurt of milk into each cup. He took two eggs out of the box and broke them into the pan; then, after a moment's hesitation, he broke a third egg into the pan.

'Walls is always hungry for his supper on a Saturday night, after the drink,' he murmured. 'What a man for eggs!'

The Troubling of the Waters

There is much talk lately about Quoylay whisky, but the truth is, there were several different kinds of whisky in that island.

Tom of Seatter's whisky was like a blowlamp flame in your throat, the reason being that there was no Seatter tradition of whisky-making; Tom merely scavenged odds and ends of technical information from here and there. Two excisemen caught him making it in his barn. He was fined a hundred pounds in the Sheriff Court and all his implements were confiscated. There was still a bottle or two of Seatter whisky in the hill crofts last winter, but nobody really liked it. You had to drink the well dry to take the scald out of your throat next morning.

Nobody ever got a chance to taste Paul Baikie's whisky, because he and his three sons – dark unpopular men – drank it all themselves. It can't have been good whisky, because when they were drunk the Baikie men were more morose than ever. Nobody can deny they were very fine boatmen. It's said Roland the tramp informed on them, after he had got nothing but a cup of sour milk out of them one cold winter day. Paul Baikie refused to pay the fine. He was in jail a whole summer.

Perhaps the most famous whisky in Quoylay was made by a henwife called Beena Bews. It was made to an ancient fixed recipe, a traditional thing like a ballad that had salted the life of generations. It wet the lips of new-born babies and old dying men in every corner of the island, and it was an essential ingredient in the bride's cog at a wedding. I tasted it once; it wasn't good. Beena Bews is dead now, and that ancient ballad is lost.

The tinkers of Voes made a whisky. I would rather not speak about it. It was made apparently without vessels of any kind, but wrung out of cloths heavy with distillation. John the tinker was blind from it when he was twenty-seven. That whisky is not made any more.

Noah Folster made a whisky that was appreciated in cultured quarters. The laird said he could taste the peat of Keelylang in it. Mr Seward the teacher detected the unique loamy flavour of Quoylay grain, every sip (he said) lapped his tongue like a yellow wave of harvest. Mr McVey the minister said an empty jar of Noah Folster was like the death of a brilliant young poet . . . With all that fulsome talk in high circles Noah was quickly in trouble. The laird paid his fine, and so he should have – all that palaver about the fragrance of buried forests! Noah's whisky was the colour of dirty daylight, and its taste on my palate was bogwater with an evil essence in it. Noah went on making the stuff for many a day after that, in the laird's cellar, behind a double-locked door.

Sweyn Johnstone went into his outhouse one morning, poured the half-distilled spirit into the burn, took a great hammer and systematically beat his copper still into a burnished lump. It was the finest still in the island, the old men say, a work of art made by the present blacksmith's great-grandfather in 1821 to the order of Captain Fenwick of the *Beagle* . . . Sweyn's wife, out feeding the hens, had seen the excisemen walking up the hill. It turned out to be the new minister, not the exciseman at all. Sweyn went into the house, drank tea with the new minister and spoke civilly for an hour about politics and the weather. He never made whisky after that day. They say the ducks in his burn were drunk for a week.

Deaf Check's whisky had a promising taste, but it was always drunk too new. 'Very old Orkney whisky,' Check used to say to the ploughmen who visited him on a Saturday night, but in fact it was never more than six or seven weeks old. It was the colour of winter sunlight. Nobody ever informed on Check. Ten years after he was dead a stone jar of his whisky was found under the brig-stone at his front door that was being repaired. 'Never, never, never was there stuff like it,' said Jacob Robb, the mason who found it, a man not given to exaggeration. 'I lived,' he said, 'in the Island of the Young, an enchanted man for three days until that stone jar was dry.'

*

Nowadays there is a licensed grocer at the cross-roads, a Mr MacFarlane from Dalkeith, where the island people buy their whisky in sealed bottles at two pounds one shilling and sixpence a bottle.

The Ferryman

At noon on Martinmas day, disinherited, I left Mirdale –
my brother's wife sending her spiteful mirth after me
across three fields, and the old man cold with spite in his
grave – and turned my steps in the direction of the Hall.
The factor could offer me one job only, to row the boat
Lupin between the island and the town with any passen-
gers who might wish to cross.

At that time of year, the threshold of winter, Hoy Sound
is often stormy, crammed with wave and squall, and a tide
runs broken and abrupt from the Atlantic into Scapa Flow
and back again, twice a day.

I agreed to take charge of the boat until such time as Joe
the ferryman recovered from his broken leg.

The next morning I waited a while at the rock,
smoking, before anybody came. A man walked along
the beach with his face muffled and ordered me to take
him across. I looked into the suffering eyes of Josie of
Taing.

'I have the toothache in my jaw,' he said, 'and no man
in this island can pull the rotten tooth out. My teeth are
too deep in my skull. But they say the blacksmith in
Stromness has fingers like nut-crackers.'

I rowed Josie across for sixpence.

At the pier of Stromness were three girls with a basket of herring who wanted to sell their fish in the island.

They were helping each other aboard the *Lupin*, chattering like starlings, when a dark hooded man walked down the slip and said: 'Behold, is this the ferry to the wicked Godforsaken island across the firth?'

When the three girls saw the black Bible under his arm they scrambled back on to the pier; for it is and always has been a thing of small luck to travel on the sea with a preaching man.

The preacher did not open his mouth all the way across. He sat in the stern and read his Bible. I didn't care for the look of the man. He didn't offer to pay his fare, and to tell the truth I was afraid to ask him. Still thumbing his Bible he stepped ashore and went swaying up the beach over the slippery stones. 'May your preaching prosper,' I shouted after him. 'It's a wicked island you've come to, and be sure to visit the croft of Mirdale. The worst woman in Orkney lives there.'

I sat on the thwart till noon smoking my pipe and nodding, and then didn't the two hawkers who have been scrounging and threatening and stealing their way through Hoy and Flotta and Graemsay since the middle of October come up to me as silent as otters. 'Take us to Stromness,' said the man.

'Sixpence each,' I said.

'We're poor wandering people,' said the woman. 'I have the black cough in my throat this week past.'

'A shilling for the two,' I said, 'if that sounds any better.'

'You have an unlucky look about you,' said the man. 'It isn't likely you'll see age.'

'Half a florin,' I said, 'and that's as low as I'll come.'

All the way across they sat in the bow muttering to each other, and every now and then sending a black look across at me.

At last they stood on the steps at Stromness pier, and the hawker woman turned to skirl at me as sharp as a gull, 'May your boards fall asunder in the middle of Hoy Sound, and may the mouth of the shark be under you that day!'

The three herring girls ran down the pier out of the pub, red in the face with porter. They scrambled on board the *Lupin* with shrieks and grey flurries of skirt. Their names were Margaret, Annie and Seenie. They laughed most of the way across the Sound. Seenie took a half-bottle of rum from her skirt pocket and we all began to drink, the flask going from mouth to mouth. Margaret was sick in the middle of the Sound. The other three of us finished the rum. Seenie threw the empty half-bottle into the tide-race. I did not charge a fare. They gave me a bunch of herring for nothing.

I sat on the beach of the island smoking, my arms so stiff with rowing I could hardly lift my pipe to my teeth. It had been a fine blue day, but now the wind turned into the east and blew grey gurls over the Sound.

At ten past three there was a plaintive outcry mixed with cursing and swearing from the road above, and then appeared Mansie of Cott dragging a grey ewe over the tangle.

'I'm taking her,' he said, 'to the butcher in Stromness, and God help me, I'm loath to part with her. She's been a good ewe and dropped a dozen fine lambs, but Jessie-Bella wants a new coat and hat for the kirk on Sabbath. Truth to tell, I would rather the ewe was safe in her field and it was Jessie-Bella I was taking to the butcher in Stromness.'

I took sixpence for Mansie's fare and threepence for the sheep.

I had hardly pushed the sharny backside of the beast off the boat when who set his boot on the rocking thwart but the Stromness police sergeant, Long Rob.

'Turn your boat round quickly, my man,' said Long Rob. 'The law's required this day in the island.' He had a blue paper, a summons, sticking out of his pocket.

By now the wind was racketing round the corners of the houses and tearing the gulls out of their clean circles.

'Is it the black preacher you're after?' I said.

'It is not,' said Long Rob.

'It wouldn't be the woman of Mirdale you're going to arrest?' I cried in sudden wild hope.

'It's Tom of Braewick,' said he, 'that must face the sheriff on Tuesday first for having no licence for his motor-bike.'

'That'll be sixpence for your fare,' I said, and I wish I had never spoken, for I had to sign my name on a form in two places – a difficult thing for me at any time – stating that I had duly received the above-mentioned sum; and the boat jumping and stotting all over the Sound with the rising rage of the sea.

By the time I set the sergeant ashore in the island the

sky was as purple as squashed grapes. I began to pull the *Lupin* up over the wet stones.

Only a fool, I thought to myself, will want to travel on a night like this! The thought had hardly shaped itself in my mind when six men came out of the gloom with a coffin on their shoulders. 'This is Williamina of Bewsley,' said Frank the undertaker. 'She's to be buried in Stromness, where she came from, tomorrow morning. If you ask me she's been in this island fifty years too long.' With that he put a sixpence on the lid of the coffin.

So I ferried Williamina of Bewsley across the waters of death. It was a black passage. Six other men were waiting at Stromness for the coffin. They lifted it without a word on to their shoulders and walked solemnly up the pier, the street lights falling dreich on to them till they turned up the close to the house where the dead woman had been born seventy years before.

Spray was flying across the harbour like smoke. I tied up the *Lupin* at the pier and slept that night on a truss of straw in the cattle shed.

I dreamt of the cornfields of Mirdale.

The Storm Watchers

A Play for Voices

A long shore. Darkness. Seven women standing.

ANNA: I am Anna. The name of my man is Ally. He worked among the hills with a plough and horses. I did not know him then, with the clay on his boots. There came a summer of black corn.

THE WOMEN: The rock is black and cold tonight. The holy rock, Hellyan.

MERRAG: Merrag is my name – an old woman with a grey rope of hair. I never suffered the kisses and foolish words of any man. On account of James my brother I have sour chaste hands.

THE WOMEN: The rock is long and cold tonight. Hellyan, the kirk rock.

MARGET: I am Marget. 'Who are you, Marget?' said Robbie, 'to be twisting wet shirts for five brothers? Who are you to be stirring oatmeal for them three times a day above a blink of fire? . . . But come,' he said, 'I have a boat and a net and a white lonely place above the shore.'

THE WOMEN: Hellyan is the name of this rock. A place of seals and saints and gannets. But fishermen avoid it.

KITTAG: Kittag they call me. My proper name is Catherine. I can write words and I have read a book called *Prudence* and another called *Fortitude*. I have three bonnets that I wear to the kirk, one for each season. Catherine he called me when he courted me, this Peter.

THE WOMEN: Here the gulls sit, on Hellyan, head into wind, winter and summer.

KIRSTY: Kirsty, that's myself. One morning my father said, 'Stir yourself today, a visitor is coming from the island of Westray to take your sister Mary away.' I scrubbed the board white and the floor blue. My mother put lupins in the window. Then the stranger came and sat at the board. They called him Josh. He carried the smell of the sea with him. My sisters put oatcakes and cheese and whisky before him.

THE WOMEN: Sailors steer by that landmark. A good rock on a summer day, Hellyan.

RUTH: Ruth is my name. A storm gave my Tors to me. They brought him from the tooth of the sea, a peerie black sodden man. They filled his foreign throat with whisky. They trussed him in a grey blanket. All that winter I taught him English words.

THE WOMEN: Tonight the rock is loud and cold, and dark, Hellyan.

SEENY: I am Seeny. I live with Mansie that men call the blue stallion. I am not married to him, but my three sons are his. Mansie has a lonely, barren, Bible-reading wife in the island of Hoy.

THE WOMEN: Hellyan is loud tonight. The rock of saints and grief and drowning.

*

ANNA: There came the summer of black corn. Ally left his father's croft and came down to the shore for limpets and seaweed. Anna is my name. The people of the hill were hungry that year, and the sea full of fish. My father put an oat in Ally's hand.

THE WOMEN: A knock at the door for us, near midnight.

MERRAG: On account of James my brother I have faded hands. That one has spoken to no woman for forty winters, not to me even, though he mumbles long to God over the broken bread. Yet this morning he said, 'The west is rough.' And at the door he said, 'We are poor people, we must fish.' My name is Merrag. James has a thousand shillings, white and grey, in a box under his bed. Then he turned and walked down to the shore.

THE WOMEN: Yet we were not asleep.

MARGET: 'I have a boat,' said Robbie, 'and a net, and a white lonely place above the shore.' The way he would turn a bit of tarry twine in upon itself with his witty fingers, and knot it, and throw the ordered holes out in every direction to be a trap for fishes, a net, a dark shroud! Marget they call me. Stars swarmed across my bride window like sillocks.

THE WOMEN: We lit oil lamps in the window.

KITTAG: Catherine he called me when he courted. me, this Peter. Catherine is my proper name, Then one morning

in March he said, 'Kathy, put the cuithes in salt,' and a
summer day he filled my white hands with cod's liver:
'Kittag, squeeze the oil into the lamps.' Before a year
was out I had more kicks than kisses from him, and the
only words I had time to read for baking, brewing,
spinning, darning, gutting fish, was the shorter cate-
chism. This Peter was an elder. And 'Kittag, Kittag,
Kittag,' the neighbours called me all along the shore.
But Catherine is my proper name.

THE WOMEN: We put shawls on our heads.

KIRSTY: They laid oatcakes, cheese and whisky before Josh.
'Over there by the fire is our eldest daughter Mary,' said
my father, but it was me Josh looked at, breaking his
oatcake. 'Here now is our second daughter Sarah at the
kirn,' said my mother, but Josh looked only at me,
cutting his cheese . . . 'Peerie Kirst is too young for a
man,' they said both together, but Josh drank his
whisky and bent forward till the light from his grey
eyes fell on me alone in all that clucking house.

THE WOMEN: We tugged at our shaking doors.

RUTH: All that winter I taught my Tors to speak English
words. The children would run in terror from his
foreign face; the fishermen were surly at him, till the
day he brought the *Solan* home, crammed with haddocks, through a blind snow-storm. Ruth they call me.
One night my father put our hands together, Tors with
Ruth, and my brother sailed across the Sound next
morning with a wedding fee to the minister.

THE WOMEN: Shorewards we leaned, one by one.

SEENY: The blue stallion has a barren Bible-reading wife in

the island of Hoy. We must be gentle and not complain too much. I trust that woman in Hoy is praying for Mansie this dark morning. And for me too. I do not wish to be an enemy of God. It is true I am a whore and a bad woman. I am on my knees here, watching the dark water for sight of bodies. I am no friend of God and this morning he is no friend of mine. Yet I wish the friend of God would pray for me, and for Mansie, and for all the men on the boat and for the women on the shore. I am afraid of the noise out there, at the rock, where wind and ebb are meeting with a black noise.

THE WOMEN: The night was dark, a shut oyster.

*

The bodies come ashore.
One by one the women kneel down.

ANNA: The people from the hill will come now, Ally, and carry you back, and lay you among their old corn dead. What it is, one cold sea kiss! I think I will not forget Ally, whose ploughman's hand was clumsy with hook and oar.

THE WOMEN: Lord, have mercy on us.

MERRAG: What do you want me to do now, sew your thousand shillings in your shroud? For forty years you said not a word. Now you'll be quiet all time. And I thought you said too many words last morning, you drowned old silent man, James my brother.

THE WOMEN: Lord, have mercy on us.

MARGET: All I can do for you now, Robbie, is carry you up the beach and through the door and lay you on the flagstones and take the seaweed out of your hair and strip the oozing clothes from you and wash the salt from your body and put the long grey shirt on you and set out the whisky bottle and twelve glasses for the mourners and send word to the grave-digger and sing to the cradled bairn, 'Sleep on, your father's late to-night, he's out beyond Hoy where the mermaids are, and the whales, and the drowned ships.'

THE WOMEN: Lord, have mercy on us.

KITTAG: Thank goodness, I have decent black clothes in the kist, and a black hat with a black ribbon on it. Out of the insurance money Peter will get a black coffin and a deep black grave and a stone with black letters on it. What a black company will follow the hearse over the hill! Is it better to be the widow-woman Catherine than Kittag the fisherman's wife? It's doucer, a respectable thing, and I'll never once put my hands in salt again, no never.

THE WOMEN: Lord, have mercy on us.

KIRSTY: Josh, you named the seven stars for me. You showed me the kittiwake's hall in the crag. 'Here,' you said, 'seal-women sang to my father.'

Wanderings of whale and gannet were secrets between us,

And how the lobsters put on their hard blue coats in summer,

And cuithe come, legions long, to drink the May flood.

'There,' you said, 'is a good flat stone to weigh a creel.'

You showed me how to mend a broken net. Many good things you told me, Josh. But you did not tell me death is like this.

THE WOMEN: Lord, have mercy on us.

RUTH: Six bodies here, among the seaweed, at first light. All the shore women but myself, Ruth, has her man. The body of Tors has not come ashore. The sea is a wild lover, she'll strip Tors to the skeleton, out there in the shifting beds. I kneel on the shore, alone of seven, at a grey rock in the first light.

THE WOMEN: Lord, have mercy on us.

SEENY: I pray for Magnus, the blue sea stallion, a trouble to many women.

I pray for James with his two hoards of silver, fish and florins.

I pray for Robbie who spread his nets on a white wall.

I pray for Peter who taught Catherine the school-mistress to bake and scrub, things needful for a woman to know.

What but hunger brought Ally down from the hill? Love kept him. I pray for that quiet horseman.

I pray for Tors, the foreign skipper – twice the sea took him and once gave him back.

I pray for Josh, gentle as seals, fierce as gannets.

THE WOMEN: Lord, have mercy on them.

Lord, have mercy on us.

Eternal Fish in the salt net between the drowned and the hungry, feed our griefs.

Tam

There was once a young Orkneyman called Tam who lived with his mother in a croft among the hills. It was a poor croft, and the laird was a hard man. Many a winter morning Tam had to tramp miles to the Birsay coast to gather limpets and dulse, when there was nothing in the house to eat.

At last, one winter, things came to such a pass that Tam could endure it no longer. He decided that, as soon as spring came, he would set out for Stromness and catch a boat going to Hudson's Bay or the Davis Straits. If he stayed in the 'nor'-wast' for a few years, he reasoned with the old woman, and if he worked hard, maybe he would arrive back in Orkney with a bag of money. Then he could bury her decently among her fathers in the kirkyard and buy a new cow, and a new plough, and a new watch to wear in his waistcoat pocket on Sundays.

Lulled by these promises, the old woman consented. One morning in March, Tam tramped along the squelching road to Stromness. He carried his boots in one hand and a bundle in the other. The bundle contained two bere bannocks, a hard-boiled egg, and a Bible.

*

The harbour was full of masts when he arrived in the town, and the street was full of strange sailors and country lads, all bound like himself for the great white spaces five hundred miles over the horizon.

The first thing Tam did was to go to the agent. The agent eyed him, noting the great width of his shoulders and the shy steady light in his eyes. Then he put a quill pen in Tam's hand and told him to sign his name on a form. Tam managed it with a mighty furrowing of his brow.

'The ship sails in the morning,' said the agent. 'Where will thu sleep this night?'

'Maybe Jock, my second cousin, will tak' me in,' said Tam.

The agent patted him on the shoulder, and Tam set out to look for the house of Jock his second cousin.

*

Jock was a cobbler, who lived up a dark close. He was very religious, and had curious ideas of sin and justification. He was a widower and had three bright-eyed, apple-cheeked daughters, clustered in age round the sweet number twenty, like three wasps round a squashed plum. They worked well for Jock. They kept his house as clean as a bone. Every text was straight on the wall, not a cobweb adhering to it. When he went to the meeting on Sabbath mornings, Jock's trousers had an edge on them as sharp as death's sting. The names of these three girls were: Bella, Jamesina, and Margaret-Ann.

Now Jock was worldly enough to appreciate the good

works his three daughters did for him. He had no intention of forfeiting one jot or tittle of the comforts with which their willing hands supplied him. So young men were discouraged from coming about the house. And Bella, Jamesina and Margaret-Ann were discouraged from going out walks at night. Sometimes Jock gave them a ringing clout on the ear to drive the point home.

So the three girls resigned themselves to spinsterhood, and went back to their household tasks. But sometimes each of them, when she was alone, fetched a profound sigh from the bottom of her diaphragm.

Then Tam arrived, asking for a night's lodging.

Jock glowered at him, but took him in, for he could scarcely refuse his own second cousin.

Bella, Jamesina and Margaret-Ann, standing well back from the threshold, eyed him with looks at once sweet and shy, like doves when a child comes among them crumbling cake.

After midnight, Tam had occasion to rise from his bed, and while he was groping his way back to it in the darkness, suddenly he found himself tangled in soft warm human arms. He had gone into the wrong room, but the enchantment of his mistake forbade any retreat. He lay where he was, while the stars marched across the skylight, a great rejoicing legion. The only thing the foolish lad could say was, 'Bella . . . Bella . . . Bella.'

He was awakened from his folly by a pool of light shining on him and Bella from above. It was Jamesina, with a candle in her hand. Her eyes, though loaded with sleep, were soft and appealing.

'Tam,' she said, 'thu must come with me now, or I'll tell me father.'

Gently and firmly, Bella propelled him into Jamesina's arms, and the candle was blown out. The night was a cave of dripping sweetness, in which he lay drenched and exhausted, but exulting in the vigour and beauty of his manhood.

The first greyness of morning fumed across the skylight, and brought him back to the sadness of human existence; for he heard a low harsh weeping beside the window with the fern in it, and there sat the youngest sister Margaret-Ann with her face buried in her nightgown.

'For pity's sake,' said Jamesina, 'go now and comfort our poor peerie sister Margaret-Ann.'

So it came about, that before the sun had cleared the Orphir hills, Margaret-Ann had stopped her lamenting, and Tam went down for the third time into the deep dark waters of love, whose waves thunder forever with a wild, uncertain, joyous rhythm on the tragic shores of life.

*

Next morning Tam sailed away into the 'nor'-wast' and was never heard tell of again.

The old woman died alone in her croft among the hills. And three bonny bairns, born within a week of each other, played on the steps of the close where Jock the shoemaker lived.

Witch

And at the farm of Howe, she being in service there, we spoke directly to the woman Marian Isbister, and after laid bonds on her. She lay that night in the laird's house, in a narrow place under the roof.

In the morning, therefore, she not yet having broken fast, the laird comes to her.

LAIRD: Tell us thy name.

MARIAN: Thou knowest my name well. Was I not with thy lady at her confinement in winter?

LAIRD: Answer to the point, and with respect. Thy name.

MARIAN: I was called Marian Isbister in Christian baptism.

STEPHEN BUTTQUOY (who was likewise present and is a factor of the Earl of Orkney): And what name does thy dark master call thee?

LAIRD: What is thy age?

MARIAN: I was eighteen on Johnsmas Eve.

LAIRD: Art thou a witch?

At this, she raised her fists to her head and made no further answer.

That same day, in the afternoon, she was convoyed to

Kirkwall on horseback, to the palace of the earl there. All that road she spoke not a word. There in Kirkwall a chain was hung between her arm and the stone.

Next morning came to her Andrew Monteith, chaplain to the earl.

MONTEITH: Thou needest not fear me. I am a man in holy orders.

MARIAN: I fear thee and everyone. My father should be here.

MONTEITH: Thou hast a scunner at me for that I am a man of God and thou art a servant of the devil.

MARIAN: How can I answer thee well? They keep food from me.

MONTEITH: I will speak for food to be given thee.

MARIAN: I thank thee then.

MONTEITH: Wilt thou not be plain with me?

MARIAN: All would say then, this was the cunning of the evil one, to make me speak plain. I do speak plain, for I am no witch, but a plain country girl.

MONTEITH: Thou art as miserable a wretch as ever sat against that wall.

MARIAN: I am indeed.

MONTEITH: Thy guilt is plain in thy face.

MARIAN: John St Clair should be here.

MONTEITH: What man is that?

MARIAN: The shepherd on Greenay Hill. He would not suffer thee to say such ill words against me.

MONTEITH: Is he thy sweetheart?

MARIAN: Often enough he called himself that.

That day, at noon, they gave her milk and fish and a barley cake, the which she ate properly, thanking God beforehand. They likewise provided her a vessel for the relief of nature. It was not thought well to give her a lamp at night.

So seven days passed, a total week. On the Sabbath she prayed much. She ate little that day, but prayed and wept.

On the Tuesday came to her cell William Bourtree, Simon Leslie, John Glaitness, and John Beaton, together with the chaplain, and two clerks (myself being one) to make due note of her utterances.

MONTEITH: Stand up, witch. Thou must suffer the witch's test on thy body.

MARIAN: I think shame to be seen naked before strange men. This will be a hard thing to endure. A woman should be near me.

They bring Janet, wife to William Bourtree.

JANET: I think none of you would have your wives and daughters, no nor the beast in your field, dealt with thus.

She kissed Marian, and then unlaced her, she making now no objection.

Then the probe was put into the said Marian's body, in order to prove an area of insensitivity, the devil always honouring his servants in that style. These parts were probed: the breast, buttocks, shoulders, arms, thighs. Marian displayed signs of much suffering, as moaning, sweating, shivering, but uttered no words. On the seventh probe she lost her awareness and fell to the ground. They moved then to revive her with water.

JANET: She suffers much, at every stab of that thin knife, and yet I think she suffers more from your eyes and your hands – all that would be matter of laughter to a true witch.

Yet they still made three further trials of the probe at that session, Marian Isbister discovering much anguish of body at each insertion.

Then they leave her.

That night she slept little, nor did she eat and drink on the day following, and only a little water on the day following that. She asked much for Janet Bourtree, but Janet Bourtree was denied access to her.

On the eleventh day of her confinement a new face appeared to her, namely Master Peter Atholl, minister of the parish, a man of comely figure and gentle in his language. He, sitting companionably at the side of Marian Isbister, taketh her hand into his.

ATHOLL: Thou art in miserable estate truly.

MARIAN: I am and may God help me.

ATHOLL: I am sent to thee by my masters.

MARIAN: I have told everything about myself. What more do they want me to say?

ATHOLL: They accuse thee to be guilty of corn-blighting, of intercourse with fairies, of incendiarism, the souring of ale, making butterless the milk of good kye, and much forby.

MARIAN: No witch's mark was found on me.

ATHOLL: The point of a pin is but a small thing, and thy body a large area. Here are no cunning witch-finders who would infallibly know the spot where the finger of the devil touched thee with his dark blessing.

Whereupon, Marian Isbister answering nothing, and a

sign being given by Master Atholl, three men entered the prison, of whom the first unlocked the chain at her wrist, the second brought wine in a flask, and the third a lamp which he hung at the wall.

ATHOLL: This is in celebration of thy enlargement. Thou art free. Be glad now, and drink.

Then began Marian to weep for joy and to clap her hands.

MARIAN: I have never drunk wine, sir.

ATHOLL: This is from the earl himself. I will drink a little with thee.

Then they drink the wine together.

MARIAN: And am I at liberty to walk home tonight, a blameless woman?

ATHOLL: First thou shalt put thy mark to this paper.

MARIAN: I cannot read the writing on it.

ATHOLL: That matters nothing.

But Marian withdrew her hand from the parchment and let the quill fall from her fingers.

MARIAN: I fear you are little better than the other priest, and deceive me.

ATHOLL: You deceive yourself. Sign this paper, and all that will happen to thee is that thou shalt be tied to a cart and whipped through the street of Kirkwall, a small thing, and Piers the hangman is a good fellow who uses the scourge gently. But if thou art obdurate, that same Piers has strong hands to strangle thee, and a red fire to burn thee with, and a terrible eternity to dispatch thee into.

MARIAN: I wish I had never drunk thy wine. Take thy paper away.

Then was the chain put back on Marian Isbister's wrist,

and the lamp darkened on the wall, and Master Peter Atholl left her, a silent man to her from that day to the day of her death.

John Glaitness cometh to her the next morning, who telleth her she must stand her trial before the King's Sheriff in the hall of Newark of the Yards, that is to say, the earl's palace, on the Monday following.

MARIAN: I am content.

And she occupied herself much in the interval with apparent prayer, and the repetition of psalms, wherein she showed sharp memory for an unlettered girl.

Howbeit, she ate and drank now with relish, as one who had little more to fear or to hope for. In the days before her trial, for food she had brose, and potage, and a little fish, and milk, ale, and water for her drink, without stint.

*

Two days before the commencement of her trial, there came to Earl Patrick Stewart where he was hunting in Birsay, a deputation of men from her parish, among them a few who were mentioned in the indictment as having been damaged by her machinations, namely, George Taing whose butter-kirn she had enchanted, Robert Folster whose young son she had carried to the fairies on the hill, Adam Adamson whose boat she had overturned whereby two of his three sons were drowned, these and others came to the earl at the shore of Birsay, protesting that they had never at any time laid information against Marian Isbister as having harmed them or theirs, but they knew on the contrary the charge was a devised thing by Stephen Buttquoy, a factor of the earl, for that his lustful advances to the girl Marian Isbister in the byre at Howe (Stephen Buttquoy riding round the parish at that time for the collection of his lordship's rents) had gotten no encouragement. Nor had there wanted women in the parish, and a few men also, to infect the bruised pride of Stephen Buttquoy with dark suggestions concerning the girl, out of malice and envy.

This deputation the earl heard fairly and openly, and he promised to investigate their words and allegations – 'and yet,' says he, 'Master Buttquoy is my good and faithful servant, and I will not easily believe him to be guilty of such an essayed wrenching of justice. And, furthermore, the woman is in the hands of the law, whose end is equity and peace, and doubtless if she is innocent not a hair of her head will suffer.'

*

The day before her trial she sat long in the afternoon with Janet Bourtree.

MARIAN: It is the common thing to be first a child, and then a maiden, and then a wife, and then perhaps a widow and an old patient woman before death. But that way is not for me.

JANET: There is much grief at every milestone. A young girl cries for a lost bird. An old woman stands among six graves or seven in the kirkyard. It is best not to tarry overlong on the road.

MARIAN: Yet with John the shepherd I might have been content for a summer or two.

JANET: Yea, and I thought that with my barbarian.

Now they bring her to trial in the great hall of the palace. There sat in judgment upon her the Sheriff, Master Malachi Lorimer. The procurator was Master James Muir. Merchants and craftsmen of the town of Kirkwall, fifteen in number, sat at the jurors' table.

The officers had much ado to keep out a noisy swarm of the vulgar, as carters, ale-house keepers, ploughmen, seamen, indigents, who demanded admittance, using much violent and uproarious language in the yard outside. And though it was the earl's desire that only the more respectable sort be admitted, yet many of those others forced a way in also. (That year was much popular disorder in the islands, on account of the earl's recent decree concerning impressed labour, and the adjustment of weights and measures, whereby certain of the commonalty claimed to be much abused in their ancient rights and freedoms.)

Marian Isbister appeared and answered 'Not guilty' to the charge in a low voice. Then began Master James Muir to list against her a heavy indictment, as burning, cursing net and plough, intercourse with devil and trow, enchanting men, cows, pigs, horses, manipulation of winds in order to extract tribute from storm-bound seamen, and he declared he would bring witnesses in proof of all.

Jean Scollite, widow in Waness, witness, said Marian

Isbister walked round her house three times against the sun the night before the Lammas Market, whereby her dog fell sick and died.

Oliver Spens, farmer in Congesquoy, witness, said he was on the vessel *Maribel* crossing from Hoy to Cairston, which vessel was much tossed by storm all the way, whereby all except Marian Isbister were sick and in much fear of drowning. But the said Marian Isbister said they would all doubtless come safe to the shore.

John Lyking, farmer in Clowster, witness, said his black cow would not take the bull two years. The bull was from the farm of Howe, where Marian Isbister was in service. Yet his cow at once took the bull from the farm of Redland on the far side of the hill.

Maud Sinclair, servant lass in Howe, witness, said she had a child by Robert the ploughman there, that dwined with sickness from the age of three months, and was like to die. But as soon as Marian Isbister was taken from Howe by the earl's officers, the child began to recover.

THE SHERIFF: And is thy child well now?

MAUD SINCLAIR: It is buried these six days, and never a penny did I have from Robert the ploughman, either for the lawless pleasure he had of me, nor for the bairn's nurse-fee, nor for the laying-out and burial of the body. And but that I am told to say what I do, I have no complaint against Marian Isbister, who was ever a sweet friend to me and loving to the child.

THE SHERIFF: This is idle nonsense. Step down.

Andrew Caithness, farmer in Helyatoun, witness, said he had a fire in his haystack the very day that Marian Isbister passed that way with her black shawl coming home from the kirk. None other had passed that way that day.

MARIAN: Yet I never did thee harm, Andrew, and never till today hast thou complained of me. And did not thy leaky lantern set fire to the heather on Orphir Hill that same spring?

ANDREW: It did that, Marian.

Ann St Clair, in Deepdale, witness, said she got no butter from her churn the day she reproved Marian Isbister for kissing lewdly at the end of the peatstock her son John who was shepherd at Greenay in Birsay.

William St Clair, spouse to the above, farmer in Deepdale, witness, said he was ill at ease whenever the prisoner came about the house, which lately was more than he could abide. He had lost three sheep, and his son was held from his lawful work, and one day, all his household being in the oatfield cutting, a thick rain fell upon his field that fell nowhere else in the parish, and with the rain a wind, so that his oats were much damaged. And one day when he reproved Marian Isbister for coming so much about the place after his son, he that same night and for a week following suffered much pain in the shoulder, that kept him from work and sleep.

John St Clair, son to the above, shepherd in Greenay, witness, stated that he was a man of normal lustihood, who before he met with Marian Isbister had fathered three children on different women in the parish. Yet after he met Marian Isbister, he was unable through her enchantment to have fleshly dealings with her, though he felt deeper affection for her than for any other woman. And this he attributed to her bewitching of his members.

Margaret Gray, spinster in Blotchnie, witness, said she had known Marian Isbister to be a witch for seven years, ever since she made extracts from the juice of flowers for reddening the cheeks, eye brighteners, and sweetening of the breath.

SHERIFF: All country girls do this, do they not?

MARGARET GRAY: Yea, but Marian hath a particular art in it, and a proper skill to know the gathering-time of herbs and their true admixture.

Now the court was dismissed for eating and refreshment, and upon its reassembly The Sheriff asked Master Muir whether he had many more witnesses to call.

PROCURATOR: Upwards of a score.

SHERIFF: There is already a superfluity of that kind of evidence.

Then he asks Marian Isbister whether she wishes to speak in her defence.

MARIAN: I wished to speak, and I had much to say, but the words of John St Clair have silenced my mouth.

JANET BOURTREE: A curse on him and all the liars that have infested this court this day!

On this Janet Bourtree was removed from the court by officers.

The Sheriff then made his charge to the jury.

SHERIFF: Gentlemen, I would have you to distinguish between witchcraft and other crimes that are brought before me in this court, and God knows I am fitter to try those other crimes than the supernatural crime we are dealing with here today, for they in a sense are crimes in the natural order – that is, they have some sensible material end in view – but witchcraft involves seduction of souls and entanglements of nature, so that I would rather, as in the old days, some doctor of divinity and not I were sitting solemnly on this bench. And furthermore this devil's work displays itself under an aspect of infernal roguishness, on the mean level of jugglers and conjurers, so that the dignity of this court is sorely strained dealing with it. Yet try the case we must.

Gentlemen, I have said that straightforward crime is an ordinary enough matter. What befalls a man who steals a sheep from his neighbour? A rope is put about his neck and he is hanged; and rightly so, for by such stealing the whole economy and social harmony of the countryside is endangered. As men of property, you appreciate that.

And what becomes of a man who murders his neighbour, by knife or gun? For him also the rope is twisted and tied, and a tree of shame prepared. And rightly so, for an assassin's blade tears the whole fabric of the community. As men who uphold the sanctities of life and property, you appreciate that.

There are worse crimes still. How do we treat the man who denies the authority of his lord and seeks to overthrow it, either by cunning or by overt force? I speak not only of treason against the sovereign. There are not wanting nearer home men who murmur against the sweet person and governance of Patrick Stewart our earl.

A Voice: When will sweet Patrick restore our ruined

weights and measures? When will he leave our women alone? Sweet Patrick be damned!

At this point was taken into custody by the court officers a smallholder, Thomas Harra, who later suffered public whipping for his insolence; though many present swore that the said Thomas Harra had not once opened his mouth.

SHERIFF: You know, gentlemen, that under God we men live according to a changeless social order. Immediately under God is the King; then the lords temporal and spiritual; then knights; then craftsmen, merchants, officers, lawyers, clergymen; then at the base (though no whit less worthy in God's sight) the great multitude of fishermen, ploughmen, labourers, hewers of wood and drawers of water. Thus society appears as an organism, a harmony, with each man performing his pre-ordained task to the glory of God and the health of the whole community. He who sets himself against that harmony is worthy of a red and wretched end indeed. As loyal citizens, you appreciate that.

Such deaths we reserve for the thief, the murderer, the rebel.

Yet these criminals, though indeed they do the devil's work, are in a sense claimants on our pity, for they think, though perversely, that they are doing good. Your sheep-stealer thinks that perchance his ram could breed thick wool and fat mutton out of that grey fleece on his neighbour's hill. Your murderer undoubtedly thinks the world would be a quieter place for himself if his victim's tombstone were prematurely raised. Your rebel

(God help him) hears in his mind, through pride and arrogance, a nobler social harmony than that which obtains, for example, under our God-appointed Patrick – a sweeter concourse of pipes and lutes.

A VOICE: A piper like Patrick would have his arse kicked black and blue from every ale-house in Orkney!

On this, three more men were ejected from the court room.

SHERIFF: Today we are dealing with another kind of crime altogether, namely witchcraft.

Gentlemen, you see standing before you what appears to be an innocent and chaste girl. She has a calm honest demeanour, has she not? She could be your daughter, or mine, and we would not be ashamed of her, would we? Are not your hearts moved to pity by what you see? You would hasten to succour any woman in such parlous danger of death and the fire as she is in, and yet here, in this young person, we observe a special sweetness, a unique openness of countenance, a right winning modesty.

Gentlemen, we will not allow ourselves to be led astray by appearances.

Further, you might say, 'What is this she is accused of – changing the wind, drying the dugs of an old cow, causing a lascivious youth to be chaste? Nay (you might say) these are light derisory things, and not weighty at all in the normal scale of crime.'

Yet see this thing for what it truly is.

The souls of thief, murderer, rebel are yet in the hand of God until their last breath, but the soul of a witch is forfeit irrevocably because of the pact she has made with the Adversary.

We say this of a witch, that she is a thousand times worse than those others. She is pure evil, utter and absolute darkness, an assigned agent of hell. Of her Scripture says, *Thou shalt not suffer a witch to live.*

Regarding the apparent lightness of her misdemeanours, marvel not at that. The Prince of Darkness is not always a roaring lion, an augustitude, a harrower of the souls of men; but frequently he seeks to lure and destroy with ridiculous playful actions, like the clown or the fool at a country fair; and then, when we are convulsed with that folly, off comes the disguise, and the horn, the tail, the cloven goat hoof, the unspeakable reek of damnation, are thrust into our faces.

So, in seeming simplicity and innocence, a girl lives in her native parish. Events strange, unnatural, ridiculous, accumulate round her, too insignificant one might think to take account of. These are the first shoots of a boundless harvest of evil.

Know that evil makes slow growth in the soil of a God-ordained society. But it is well to choke the black shoots early. For if we neglect them, then in the fullness of time must we eat bitter dark bread indeed – blasphemy, adultery, fratricide, tempest, flood, war, anarchy, famine.

As men of God I ask you to consider these things, and to reach now an honest verdict in the secrecy of your chamber.

It was no long time when the jury came back with the one word *Guilty.* Then rose from his place the dempster.

DEMPSTER: Marian Isbister, for this thy crime of witch-craft proven against thee in this court, thou shalt be taken tomorrow to Gallowsha, and at the stake there strangled till no breath remains in thee, and afterwards thy body shall be burnt to ashes and scattered to the winds, and this is pronounced for doom. May the Lord have mercy on thy soul.

CHAPLAIN: Amen.

Then was Marian Isbister taken down to her prison. And at once came to her William Bourtree, Simon Leslie, John Glaitness and John Beaton, with shears, razors, and pincers, who cut off her hair and afterwards shaved her skull clean, denuding her even of her eyebrows. Then one by one with the pincers John Glaitness drew out her finger-nails and toe-nails; and this operation caused her much pain.

Then they give her water but her bleeding fingers will not hold the cup.

They put their heaviest chain upon her and left her.

That night was with her Master Andrew Monteith the chaplain, and Master Peter Atholl the parish minister, from before midnight till dawn.

MONTEITH: This is thy last night on earth.

MARIAN: I thank God for it.

Then they sought with mild comforting words to prepare her for her end. By full confession of her fault it might be God would yet have mercy on her. Yet she answered only with sighs and shakings of her head.

ATHOLL: Only say, art thou guilty of witchcraft, yea or nay.

MARIAN: It needs must be.

MONTEITH: I think the devil would not love thee now, with thy skull bare as an egg.

MARIAN: I have much pain and much sorrow.

Then they read to her from the beginning of the Book, God's marvellous creation, the happiness of Adam in the Garden, Eve's temptation by the Serpent, the eating of the fruit, the angel with the flaming sword, Abel's good sacrifice and the red hand of Cain.

To these holy words she listened with much meekness.

Then said she: 'Tell my father the sheep Peggy knows the path down to the cliff, and he is to keep watch on her to keep her from that dangerous place. And tell him there is a sleeve still to sew in his winter shirt, but Isabel his neighbour will see to that.'

Then they read to her the ending of the Book, Revelation. And having prayed, soon after dawn they left her.

In the morning, at eight o'clock, when they came for her, she was asleep. They had to rouse her with shakings and loud callings of her name.

MARIAN: It is cold.

SIMON LESLIE: Thou will soon be warm enough.

MARIAN: Yea, and there are longer fires than the brief flame at Gallowsha.

Because her toes were blue and swollen after the extraction of the cuticles, she could not walk but with much difficulty. Therefore they bound her arms and carried her out on to the street. There was much laughter and shouting at sight of her naked head. Every ale-house in town had been open since midnight, the earl having decreed a public holiday. All night people had come into the town from the parishes and islands. There was much drunkenness and dancing along the road to Gallowsha.

As she hobbled through the Laverock with her fingers like a tangle of red roots at the end of her long white arms, and her head like an egg, some had pity for her but the voices of others fell on her in a confusion of cursing and ribaldry and mockery, so that the holy words of Master Andrew Monteith could scarcely be heard.

They came to Gallowsha by a steep ascent. There beside the stake waited Piers with a new rope in his hand. With courtesy and kind words he received Marian Isbister from her jailers, and led her to the stake.

PIERS: My hands are quick at their work. Thou hast had enough of pain. Only forgive me for what I have to do.

Marian Isbister kissed him on the hands.

At this, some of the crowd shouted, 'The witch's kiss, the witch's kiss!' But Piers answered, 'I do not fear that.'

It is usual on such occasions for the sentence to be read out first, and thereafter ceremonially executed on the body of the criminal. But the clerk had not uttered three words when Piers secretly put the rope about the neck of Marian Isbister and made a quick end. Those standing near saw her give a quick shrug, and then a long shiver through her entire body. She was dead before the clerk had finished reading from the parchment. Most of that great crowd saw nothing of the strangling.

An ale booth had been erected near the stake. Men

crowded in there till the walls bulged. Many were too drunk to get near the fire. To that burning came Neil the Juggler with his two dancing dogs, Firth with his fiddle and new ballad entitled 'The Just and Dreadful End of Marian Isbister for Sorcery', Richan the hell-fire preacher, the long-haired dwarf Mans with medicine to cure consumption, palsy, the seven poxes, toothache, women's moustaches, the squinnying eye – all of whom made great uproar at Gallowsha until the time of the gathering of the ashes into a brass box, and their secret removal to the summit of the hill Wideford.

*

That same day, in the palace of Holy Rood, Edinburgh, King James the Sixth of Scotland, acting on private information, set his seal to a paper ordering due inquiry to be instituted into alleged defalcations, extortions, oppressions, and tortures practised by his cousin Earl Patrick Stewart on the groaning inhabitants of Orkney, whereby the whole realm was put in jeopardy and the providence of God affronted.

At midnight, in the town of Kirkwall, the dancing was still going on.

Master Halcrow, Priest

An obstinate uprooted man, I write this in the Glebe of the parish of Stromness, Orkney, on a harvest evening in the year of Our Lord 1561, to make more clear in my mind the dark things that have come upon us this ten years and more, especially the dreadful thing that happened yesterday, the end and consummation of all, the final untruth. A jug of ale is at my elbow, brewed by Jean Riddach (her man is this twenty winters my servant at the Glebe and does the harvesting and ploughing). I write with a warmed body and a cold uncertain mind.

I was, until yesterday, mass-priest at Stromness in the islands. My age is near what the psalmist celebrated, seventy, that sweet secret number that opens the door into eternity. My kirk, St Peter's, is built above the rocks at the shore. My people are fishermen and crofters. A few women come to my Mass each morning, and when I confess to God at the altar, to these also I confess – I fish too long at the rock, I pray only a little, I drink too much of the dark ale that they brew on the hill.

Last winter before Yule, the canon came on his rounds. He has this living but resides in Kirkwall so that he may fulfil his duties as precentor in the Cathedral of St Magnus there. (My lord the bishop troubles the lonely places but little.) The canon told me there was a new queen in Scotland, out of France, Mary her name (Our Lady, pray for her). 'Bloody times,' said the canon, 'bloody days indeed, and dour stickit men in the high places of Scotland, heretics and upstarts . . .' And what would an old priest, one who fishes and drinks too much, know about that? I inquired no more into the matter.

The canon rode away on his mare, still wagging his head in disapproval of the times.

St Peter the fisherman, pray for the Church. Our Lady of the sea, pray for the Church, that it does not shipwreck in this age. Who am I to accuse, a priest that fishes and drinks too much? (And even so I hope for a great host of cuithe to be at the rock tonight – my line is ready with six hooks and bits of whitemaa feather for lure.) Yet this I must record, though I shrink from it. Magnus Anderson, curate in Sandwick, lives and eats and sleeps with a huge woman called Angela – much laughter and lewd winks and silence in the parishes on that account. Jerome Clements in Hoy (this I know for truth) has not said Mass since the Feast of the Assumption in August. In Stenness John Coghill gabbles his Latin like a duck, yet because he is bastard son to the prebend's cousin, a place therefore had needs be found for him. St Magnus, pray for the Church. Pray for an old man whose throat is dry, though not with praying. And pray also for the good and worthy priests that are everywhere in the islands, true guardians of the Word. Easy it is to write of wickedness; their goodness is hidden with God.

There was lately a man come to the town of Kirkwall that preached under the sky like a friar, his texts the Scarlet Woman and Anti-Christ and the Whore of Babylon out of the Apocalypse. This man was not licensed by the bishop. Yet many heard him. There was shrieking, babbling, seeing of visions and speaking in tongues. Men sobbed and declared their sins openly in the streets. The bishop took no steps to control this false pretender to primitive truth, who presently went north to the outer islands and on into Shetland. The blasphemous clowning came to an end. Yet why did this thing, while it lasted, fill me with such dread, as if it was the shadow of an immense oncoming evil?

*

I had nine haddocks in my hand, a cold silver bunch like a silent bell, climbing the rocks with gulls all about me, when a solitary horseman rode over Innertun into my view. (This was the time of tall green corn, before the last burnish comes upon it and the heavy ears droop.) I saw at once who this horseman was, the bishop. He had a grave white look on him. He is a priest of much learning in the tongues – Scots, Latin, Gaelic, English, French, Greek, Italian. I have heard his sermons are deep subtle utterances, things of form and beauty, but I have never been to the Cathedral Kirk of St Magnus since my ordination fifty years ago and so I have no knowledge of his preaching. I like a sermon to be plain and wholesome like a bannock to hungry men, such as Jerome Clements used to preach in

Hoy before he ceased to say Mass and took to reading German and Swiss books.

His lordship eyed the fish and said, 'This kirk is well called St Peter's.' Then with much gravity he said he did not know how what he must now say would affect such an old man as myself – Master Anderson and Master Clements had heard it unmoved. 'My lord,' I said, 'in truth I fish and drink too much.'

'Leave that alone,' he said. 'I have no power over you any more.'

'You are my bishop,' I said.

'There are no bishops in Scotland now,' he said. 'The old kirk is put away. There is a new kirk in the land.'

'Old kirk?' I said. 'New kirk? I know but one Kirk, that which Our Lord founded.'

'It seems that now we must believe otherwise,' said the bishop.

'Who bids us believe otherwise?' I said. 'Is it the Pope?'

'No,' said the bishop. 'The Government of Scotland has passed a law. The Pope's authority is put down. All bishops and priests are abolished, and also the Mass. Relic and image and altar must be removed at once from our kirks. The word of God is become the sole guide. Every man will discover the truth that his own soul requires in holy scripture. Henceforth every man is his own priest.'

'The priesthood abolished?' I said. 'This is droll talk. I was told at the time of my first becoming a priest that I was a priest forever in the stream of the apostolic succession, and can any men of the temporality take this title from me? This was never told me before, your grace, either by you or by your predecessor that ordained me, may God keep his soul in peace.'

The bishop's face was a total flush from brow to chin. 'You must not call me "your grace" any more,' he said in a low voice. 'I am no more a bishop. Things are thus in Scotland now. We cannot alter it. They are powerful and angry men that rule in the land.'

There was silence between us then for a little while.

I then said that this was the only place I knew, and where would I and the other Orkney priests go?

'The new kirk,' said the bishop, 'will have need of ministers. You will be asked to bide where you are. Like enough you will have more money in your purse, and a louder voice in the ordering of the parish, and new freedoms, whereby for example celibacy will not be enforced and you will be able to take a woman in marriage.'

'The new kirk is kind to an old man who has been used to silence for fifty years,' I said with as much mockery and bitterness as I could infuse into my voice. 'Tell me, your grace, what will Master Anderson and Master Clements and Master Coghill do?'

'They have all three abandoned their priesthood,' said the bishop, 'together with most of the clergy of Orkney. They will adhere as ministers to this new kirk. Master Anderson was married this very morning to the fat woman that looks after his goats.' (This about goats I took to be a figurative expression, signifying inordinate lust, since Master Anderson has at no time kept goats.) Another brief silence fell between us.

I then asked the bishop what he himself would do, now that the wolf was in the sheepfold and the ravening had begun.

'I am not brave enough to be a martyr,' he said curtly. 'Tell me, Master Halcrow, what will you do?'

I said that I did not know. Here I was and here like enough I would sit until God's will in the matter was made plain.

Then the bishop rose to his feet and pressed my hand and left the Glebe. I have not seen him again.

*

Yesterday began the cutting of the oats at the Glebe. The kirk lay like a foundering ship in long windy surges of corn. The first thing I saw when I looked out at the door was John Riddach my servant sharpening his blade on a red whetstone at the end of the barn.

After Mass (the usual women were there, seven of them, with heads covered) came three strangers into the kirk, to whom I (putting out the candles) remarked that they were too late, the Mass was over for that morning, but they were welcome to bide in the kirk for as long as they liked. In truth I was anxious to get down to my boat, there being mackerel in Hoy Sound that day. 'The Mass is over,' I told them.

'The Mass is over forever,' said one of the men.

The second man drew a writ from his pocket which I saw bore the bishop's seal. 'I am Master Esson, notary from Kirkwall,' he said, 'and this young gentleman,

Master Heddle, is newly appointed minister in this re-
formed kirk. You are commanded to hand over the keys
to him at once.'

'The Mass is damnable idolatry,' said the third man in a
familiar voice. I looked closer at him, and behold it was
Magnus Anderson the Sandwick priest, the same which
had kept the woman Angela in concubinage five years and
was now her unsanctified spouse.

I then said very tartly to Master Anderson that he had
been a long time finding out that the Mass was (as he
termed it) damnable idolatry, and then, the sharpness
increasing in my voice, I took leave to congratulate with
him upon his new estate of matrimony, which was indeed
a singular state for a man who had sworn before God to
observe life-long chastity.

I turned then to the other men and said that the keys
were in my keeping and I would never give them over
unless by order of the bishop. Then they showed me the
bishop's writ, with his commands and wishes clearly set
out. Thereupon with no more ado I made over the keys to
them.

They waited for me to leave the kirk.

I bade them look well to the building, for it was a place
dear to me, I having been a priest here fifty years until
now. Every stone was become precious to me. Some of the
stones on the pavement are from the beach, I told them,
and these stones shine with wetness like dark mirrors
when there is a dampness in the atmosphere, for then
those stones (as it seems) remember the element of water
out of which they have been taken. And yet, I said, great

pity it were to remove these stones, for so lying juxtaposed with the dry stones from the quarry, they seemed to show forth the intertwining elements in this parish, sea and soil, the fish and the cornstalk, and indeed St Peter our patron had himself been a fisherman who doubtless often came wet from the sea to his prayers. And did not the very name Peter mean stone, permanence, unassailability?

Doubtless I would have spoken much more, to gather my squandered senses and delay my expulsion from the place, but Master Magnus Anderson turned to his companions and remarked anent me, 'This one always was and ever will be to his dying day a garrulous long-winded old man. Once launched on some topic like sillock-fishing or the five various ways of brewing ale, he becomes a weariness of the flesh.'

On this, there stirred in me and roused itself and presently raged that third beast of hell among the seven beasts, Wrath, and I said to Master Magnus Anderson directly concerning his long entertaining of the sixth beast of hell, Lust, (yet never does one beast cancel out another, and herein I erred grievously) – 'I trust that Mistress Angela is well,' I said. 'She is an immense piece of territory, your Newfoundland, but doubtless in time you will be able to chart the geography of her to your satisfaction, and wring much fruitfulness out of her, Father.'

He who now had charge of the parish, the new minister, fearing violence, came between us and said beseechingly that now it was time for me to go.

Thereupon I bowed my knee to the altar where lay the

Body of Our Lord and turned my back on those men and
left the kirk.

*

I walked along the coast with a blank beating mind, having
now no secure place in the world, for certain it seemed to
me that they would take from me also the Glebe and my
furrows and boat. Near noon I sat down near the edge of
the cliff (called the Black Craig) to rest me. There the
seabirds circled and fell, gleaning the waves for food. Now
came this fragment of the Word into my mind, that had
been the Gospel of the Sunday preceding:

> Behold the birds of the air, for they neither sow, nor do
> they reap, nor gather into barns, and your heavenly
> Father feedeth them. Are not you of much more value
> than they?

And scarcely the last word was remembered when this
desolation came suddenly into my mind, a thing I had
clean forgot in the kirk in my rage and grief – the *Blessed
Sacrament*! What might such men do to the Bread of
Heaven, seeing that for them now it was no longer the
Body of Our Lord but mortal bread over which five
invalid words had been uttered?

I turned back over the fields, taking the bird's path to
the kirk. Yet it was not like a bird that I went, rather it was
like an old wounded beast, hard beset, that groaned and
laboured under the yoke. John Riddach was in the oat-

field, making bright circles with his scythe. And presently, the last breath it seemed guttering in my mouth, I came again to the kirk and went in at the door.

There a shameful thing had been done. They had thrown down the statues of Our Lady and Saint Peter and Saint Magnus. The crucifix lay broken at the base of the font (agony upon agony). The stones were pale with smashed candles. I looked wildly round for the white circles of the Host to be scattered about the place but (thanks be to God!) there was no such thing, though the tabernacle stood open.

The notary shouted, 'That one is back again, the old windbag is back! Were you not well admonished to quit this place forever? Have you not wrought disgrace enough in this place, with your drunkenness and your idleness?'

'Not to speak of his idolatry and blasphemy,' said Angela's man.

The young minister, my successor (yet where was the succession? it was rather a total uprooting) said in a voice that was all delusive hope, 'It may be that Master Halcrow wishes to join our congregation. That would be a thing pleasing to us all.'

'No,' I said. 'I wish to speak with this priest, Master Anderson.'

'There is no such thing as priest any more,' said the lawyer. 'Give him his proper title.'

'Say quickly what you want,' said Master Magnus Anderson. 'Here I am.'

'I must speak with you alone,' I said.

Master Anderson shuffled his feet and looked uneasily

about him, like a dog that hears contrary orders and does not well understand either the one or the other, or where to turn his head.

Then after a short consideration the young minister said, 'You can have private talk with him for as long as it takes to utter a short psalm.' Thereupon he took the lawyer by the arm and both left by the front door, the lawyer looking back over his shoulder very ill-pleased.

I said quickly to Master Anderson, 'The Blessed Sacrament.'

Master Anderson smiled. He opened his coat. He drew from an inner pocket the bright pyx. With trembling hands he put It into my trembling hand. Then he bent forward and kissed me on the cheek. 'Pray for me, Master Halcrow,' he said. 'Pray for me. I was intending to consume It myself.'

'I will, Magnus,' I said, 'both before and after my death . . .' Then I spoke with him briefly concerning my death. 'I feel the ripeness and the rot of it inside me,' I said. 'I beg that you will come to me with the oil when you hear that I am on my last bed, either openly or in secret.'

We heard the returning shuffle of feet at the door.

'I will come in secret,' said Master Anderson.

The lawyer came back first into the kirk.

I said in a loud voice, 'I much regret what I said earlier concerning Mistress Anderson. Every body, however gross, is a temple of the Holy Ghost, and I did ill to describe it in those obscene terms.'

Master Anderson gave a bitter smile. The minister came back into the kirk. The lawyer said, 'Go now. We have much work to do in this place before it is a fit temple of the Lord and no more a temple of Baal.'

I turned my back on them – *Domine, non sum dignus –* and I put the round white circles of the Host into my mouth.

Thus transfixed, I crossed myself and walked out of the kirk. The stooks were rising bright in every field. There were two fishing boats off the Graemsay rocks. Jean Riddach was at the well with her bucket.

Saint Peter, pray for us.

The Ballad of the Rose Bush

Margaret was the name of a girl who lived in Dale with her mother and two brothers. This girl was dumb from birth. They kept her indoors; few men ever saw her; maybe Clod the shepherd and the tinkers and the men who came to the hill in summer to shoot.

Sometimes, very early, Margaret would go out by herself to the well for a bucket of water. Once she was seen up at the hill, spreading peats to dry at the peat bank.

She was said to excel at embroidering linen cloths. Other women could make little patterns of flower and shell on their cloths, but this girl sewed fish, hawks, plough-horses, so that when there was a draught between the spread cloth and the wall it seemed that the animals moved and danced on the wind.

One day in summer the women of Dale said, 'It is time for some of our peats to be taken home.'

Tom said it was impossible that particular day, because he had promised to fleece the sheep at Feolquoy, where Simon the farmer was confined to bed with a broken leg.

Sand said, 'Perhaps tomorrow. Cuithe and mackerel are thick in the Sound. By tomorrow they will be gone.'

Margaret said nothing but took the straw basket on her back and went out.

The woman of Dale said, 'There should be somebody with her.'

Tom took his shears from the wall and went out, singing.

Later she said, 'I heard music in the hills last night. The tinkers are camped there. Mick, the young tinker, has made a new reel called "The Rose Bush".'

Sand pushed his boat down over the stones.

Clod the shepherd crossed the hill at noon.

That night Tom came home with a shilling from Simon of Feolquoy for fleecing six sheep.

Tom said, 'Where's the girl?'

'She hasn't come back from the peat bank,' said the old woman.

Sand came home with wet boots. He hung the gutted cuithes in the chimney-piece among grey smoke.

'Where's Margaret?' he said.

'She isn't home yet,' said the woman of Dale.

Later she said, 'Mick, the young tinker, went down by with two dogs in the afternoon, going to the ale-house.'

'We will look for her now,' said Tom.

They searched for a long while. Then it got dark. They went on searching. They groped through the quarry and put their arms in the cold burn. Then the moon got up. At midnight Sand found her near the well of Kellyan. There was blood round her mouth and her clothes were torn. Sand lifted her over his shoulder. 'Maybe she'll still be alive when I get her home,' he said to Tom. 'Where will you go?'

'To the tinkers' camp,' said Tom.

The tinkers were sitting round a peat fire, singing among the broken light. 'Where did you get those peats?' said Tom to the old tinker. He lifted a peat and broke it. It opened blue-black and dry.

'Mick found them on the hill,' said the old tinker.

'They're our peats,' said Tom. 'Where is Mick?'

'Drunk,' said the old tinker. 'He went to sell a tin pail at the Manse to get money for more rum. He lost his fiddle on the hill.'

Tom turned away into the darkness. The tinkers began to sing where they had left off.

Tom met Mick on the road between the Manse and the ale-house. He had a half-empty bottle in one pocket and some coppers in his fist. He was going more in the ditch than on the road.

'You have blood on your jacket,' said Tom.

'That's no wonder at all,' said Mick. 'The rabbit in the snare was soaked in blood when I lifted it out this morning.'

'Did you meet anybody on the hill today?' said Tom.

'I met Clod the shepherd,' said Mick. 'He's a desperate dull man. We went round each other in a wide circle.'

'Where did you get the Dale peats?' said Tom.

'The whole hillside was scattered with them,' said Mick. 'A fine treasure on a black cold night.'

Then Tom took hold of Mick and twisted his arms behind him and tied them with a piece of rope. 'It would give me pleasure to kill you myself,' he said, 'but why should I, when there's a hangman paid for doing that job.'

Tom dragged Mick down to the smithy. There Grund the blacksmith helped him to frogmarch the tinker to the laird's house, a mile further on.

And before morning the sheriff-clerk in Kirkwall was writing out the crime on long curling parchment.

*

Meantime Sand carried Margaret home. 'There's no saying whether she'll live or die,' he said to the old woman. 'But someone will pay for this, no doubt.'

They laid the girl on her bed. For three days she neither moved nor ate. On the fourth day she sat an hour by the fire and took some warm milk.

'She'll live,' said Sand.

'And that's a pity,' said the old woman, 'for now everything's turned sour on her.' She led the girl back to her bed.

*

They hanged Mick the tinker at Gallowsha in Kirkwall three days before Christmas. He was nineteen years old that winter.

There was snow on the ground. Mick hung from the gallows a day and a night. Before dawn on the second morning the tinkers came and cut him down. They buried him in a secret place among the hills.

*

The girl Margaret never went out again. She was not able to work properly from the day they found her near the well of Kellyan, neither to churn nor brew nor bake nor spin. She never stirred to fetch water from the well. She did not weep one tear when the old woman died.

She lived twenty years after that. The winter of her death she took linen and needles and thread and she sat beside the fire a whole day sewing. She sewed black thorns with a red rose in the heart of the bush. Then she put aside the cloth, and soon after midnight she moaned and lay down on her bed. She was dead before Sand put the brandy to her mouth.

All the men of the district came to the funeral, standing round the open coffin and against the walls and crowding in the door. They stood silent, waiting for the minister.

Then the tinkers came.

The old tinker said to Tom, 'I've come here out of grief for your sister, in spite of the trouble that has been between our people in the past. I hope you will not take offence.'

'The debt was paid,' said Sand.

'We take no offence,' said Tom. 'You're welcome.'

The minister came and the funeral service began.

They carried Margaret round the shore to the kirkyard. After the burial all the mourners returned with Tom and Sand to the house for whisky and oat cakes. Only the tinkers did not come; they turned aside among the hills. The old tinker said to Tom at the cross-roads, 'They never found the fiddle. But there's always music in the hills now. You must have noticed it yourself.'

'I never noticed,' said Tom.

Then the tinkers went away.

'Men from every family in the district were at Margaret's burying,' said Grund the blacksmith to Tom and Sand. 'Your sister was well honoured.'

'Clod the shepherd wasn't there,' said Tom.

'It's too late now to create trouble,' said Sand. 'In any case, the debt has been paid.'

Now they reached Dale and the mourners all took off their grey caps and went inside one by one. A stone jar of whisky stood on the table.

'That debt was paid a long time ago,' said Tom. 'We will say no more about it.'

'No,' said Sand. 'Clod the shepherd is an old man. We are not young ourselves. There should be no trouble at this date.'

'It's known for a certainty where the tinkers buried Mick after they cut him down from the rope,' said Grund. 'They buried him in a quiet place on the side of Kringlafiold, and now there's a rose bush growing out of his grave.'

'Very likely indeed,' said Sand.

'That's a good place for him to be,' said Tom, 'but I think a man like Mick would sooner be leading his pony along the road, going to the Dounby Market on a fine morning.'

Sand carried the stone jar to the first of the mourners.

Stone Poems

Near the two lochs at the centre of Orkney rises a green hump, Maeshowe. Inside are the oldest writings in Scotland, carved with sharp edges on the walls of a burial chamber.

Seven poets took shelter in Maeshowe from a snowstorm one day in the winter of 1150; or rather, strictly speaking, there were only two professional poets, the Icelanders Arkold and Ubi, and five other Norwegians whose imaginations were suddenly quickened in that petrified womb.

The snowstorm kept them in Maeshowe most of the morning. They had been drinking new ale the night before at a farm near Hamnavoe, and they were on their way back to Kirkwall when the air turned wild and blind.

Hermund, who had been in five battles at places between Ireland and Russia, besides sieges and sackings at castles and seaports all over Europe, cut this on the wall with his blade:

HERMUND OF THE HARD AXE
CARVED THESE RUNES

Solmund was captain of the ship *Eagle* that was being repaired and caulked that winter at Scapa beach. He was one of Earl Rognvald's skippers for the crusade from Orkney to Jerusalem that would commence as soon as the ploughing was over. Solmund was a rather pious man. He hoped to swim in the River Jordan and to walk in procession along the actual Stations of the Cross between the holy city and Golgotha. He wrote this:

JERUSALEM-FARERS
BROKE IN HERE

Arkold, the Iceland poet, had fallen in love at the beginning of winter with a girl called Ingibiorg, daughter of a well-to-do farmer in Birsay. Arkold never told her or anybody about this, and even if he had it would have done him no good, for he was poor and without a patron. Yet without this silent and almost invisible girl he would not have composed all those fine verses during the crusade, and his harp would have remained the ordinary harp it usually was. Here in the stone heart of death and winter he wrote this:

INGIBIORG IS THE
MOST BEAUTIFUL
OF WOMEN

Ubi, the other Iceland poet, a mordant satirical man, looked first into the three orifices in the wall and saw the slender yellowish bones, broken rib cages, delicate skulls. Then he wrote this:

MANY A LOVELY

LADY HAS ENTERED

HERE LOW STOOPING

Bjorn, a merchant from Trondheim, said that he couldn't write, he had never learned letters, he had managed so far to conduct his business quite well without it. Yet because the name of the ship that in the past had brought him the greatest profit was the *Dragon*, a good ship and a lucky one till she foundered on a sharp Baltic rock; and because he had made a great deal of money in twelve years' trading in walrus tusks and walrus skins (thanks be to God) he would see what he could do. He cut two shapes on the wall representing a dragon transfixed by a sword, and a walrus.

Peter was captain of the *Oyster*, another ship that would sail in spring through the Mediterranean to Jerusalem, Byzantium and Rome. He was a greedy man, as tight as an oyster himself. In Maeshowe he complained all the time that they were forty years too late; the first men to break into the howe had ridden off home with rings, brooches, cairngorms and golden combs. Nothing was left now but bones and ghosts. He took up the chisel and he cut the wall in a smoor of baffled greed, till small chips of stone sang like bees around their heads:

THERE WAS AS MUCH

GOLD HERE AS COULD

BE CARRIED OFF IN THREE NIGHTS

The seventh man was Sylvanus the deacon, an elderly cleric. He had hardly tasted the ale at the Hamnavoe farm the night before when the others had drained the kirn. He had gone with them simply to see if there were any churches in the south-western part of the island. Sylvanus had thin lips when he read what Peter had written. He wrote:

IN THE NORTH-WEST

IS A GREAT TREASURE HIDDEN

'I am not referring to the trash that moth and rust devour,' he said severely. 'I am referring to the bones of the blessed Magnus that lie in the Birsay kirk ten miles north-west from this place.'

The snowflakes had stopped eddying through the torn hole in the roof of the chamber. A weak yellow light came in.

'I think,' said Peter, 'our horses will have turned their heads into the wind again.'

One by one they climbed out into the cold light.

The Story of Jorkel Hayforks

The week before midsummer Jorkel and six others took ship at Bergen in Norway and sailed west two days with a good wind behind them. They made land at Whalsay in Shetland and were well entertained at a farm there by a man called Veig. After they had had supper one of Jorkel's men played the harp and recited some verses. The name of this poet was Finn.

As soon as Finn had sat down, Brenda, the daughter of Veig the Shetlander, came to her father and said, 'Offer Finn a horse and a piece of land, so that he will be pleased to stay here.'

Veig made the offer to Finn, but Finn said, 'We are sailing to Orkney on a certain urgent matter in the morning. I can't stay.'

Veig repeated Finn's remark to Brenda.

At midnight, when the men were drinking round the fire, Brenda rose out of bed and said to her father Veig, 'I can't get to sleep. Offer Finn a gold arm-band and a silver ring to stay here in Shetland.'

Veig called Finn aside and made this offer. Finn said, 'I am a poor man and a happy man, and gold and women would distract me from the making of verses. Besides, we have an appointment to keep in Orkney on midsummer day.'

Veig told Brenda what Finn had said.

At dawn, though the ale keg was empty, the men were still sitting at the fire. Some of them were lying under the benches drunk, but Finn was discussing metres with the Shetlanders. 'I would argue better,' said Finn, 'if I was not so dry.'

Soon after that Brenda came in and offered Finn a cup of ale.

With the froth still wet on his beard, Finn turned to Brenda and said, 'Did you brew this ale, woman?' Brenda said that she alone had made it. Then Finn said, 'On account of this ale I will stay for a while with you here in Shetland.'

Then the sun got up and the Norwegians stirred themselves and went on board their ship. But Finn was nowhere to be found, and the door of Brenda's room was barred. Jorkel was very angry about that.

They say that Finn made no more poems after that day. Brenda bore him twelve children. He died there in Shetland before there was a grey hair in his beard. He was drunk most days till his death, and he would drink from no cup but Brenda's. He was totally dependent on her always. It was thought rather a pity that such a promising poet should make such an ordinary end.

'She bewitched him, that bitch,' said Jorkel.

*

In the afternoon of the same day, Jorkel's ship reached Fair Isle. They saw some sheep on a hillside there. Flan, who was a blacksmith back in Norway, said they were fine sheep. 'And my wife,' said he, 'will be looking for a present from the west. I will bring her a fleece from Fair Isle.'

Before they could stop Flan he leapt overboard and swam ashore. The sheep were grazing at the edge of a high cliff. Flan climbed up this face, disturbing the sea birds that were there, and laid hands on the first sheep he saw. He was raising his axe to despatch the ewe when another sheep ran terrified between his legs and toppled him over the edge of the crag, so that the sea birds were wildly agitated for the second time that day.

'Flan's descent is much quicker than his going up,' said Jorkel. 'What does a blacksmith know about shepherding?'

They anchored that night under the cliffs of Fair Isle.

*

They left Fair Isle at dawn and had a rough crossing to the Orkneys. There was a strong wind from the east and the sea fell into the ship in cold grey lumps, so that they were kept busy with the bailing pans.

Then Mund who had a farm east in Sweden laid down his bailing pan.

He said, 'I have made deep furrows in the land with my plough but I did not believe there could be furrows in the world like this.'

The men went on bailing.

Later Mund said, 'When Grettir lay dying in his bed at

Gothenburg last summer his face was like milk. Is my face that colour?'

Jorkel said his face was more of a green colour, and urged the men to bail all the harder, since now Mund was taking no part in the game.

At noon Mund said, 'I was always a gay man at midsummer, but I do not expect to be dancing round a Johnsmas fire this year.'

The men went on bailing, until presently the wind shifted into the north and moderated, so that they were able to cook a meal of stewed rabbit and to open a keg of ale.

But when they brought the meat and ale to Mund, they found him lying very still and cold against a thwart.

'Mund will not be needing dinner any more,' said Jorkel.

*

They reached Papa Westray soon after that. There were some decent farms in the island, and an ale-house near the shore, and a small monastery with a dozen bald-headed brothers beside a loch.

The people of the island gave them a hospitable welcome, and sold them fish and mutton, and showed them where the best wells were.

The twelve brothers trooped into the church for vespers.

After the necessary business of victualling had been transacted, the Norwegians went into the ale-house to drink.

They played draughts and sang choruses so long as there was ale in the barrel. Then, when the keeper of the ale-house was opening a new barrel, Jorkel noticed that Thord was missing.

'He will have gone after the women of Papa Westray,' said Sweyn. Thord was known to be a great lecher back home in Norway.

The church bell rang for compline.

There was some fighting in the ale-house when they were midway through the second barrel, but by that time they were too drunk to hurt each other much. When things had quietened down, Jorkel remarked that Thord was still absent.

'No doubt he is stealing eggs and cheese, so that we can vary our diet on the ship,' said Valt. Thord was a famous thief on the hills of southern Norway, when it was night and everyone was sitting round the fires inside and there was no moon.

They went on drinking till the lights of yesterday and tomorrow met in a brief twilight and their senses were reeling with ale and fatigue.

'This is a strange voyage,' said Jorkel. 'It seems we are to lose a man at every station of the way.'

They heard the bell of the church ringing. Jorkel went to the door of the ale-house. Thirteen hooded figures passed under the arch to sing matins.

Jorkel returned to the ale-barrel and said, 'It seems that Thord has repented of his drinking and whoring and thieving. Yesterday there were twelve holy men in Papa Westray. This morning I counted thirteen.'

He lay down beside his companions, and they slept late into the morning.

*

Now there were only three men on the ship, Jorkel and Sweyn and Valt.

'We will not stop until we reach Hoy,' said Jorkel. 'Every time we stop there is one kind of trouble or another.'

They were among the northern Orkneys now, sailing through a wide firth with islands all around.

It turned out that none of the three knew where exactly Hoy was.

Sweyn said, 'There is a man in that low island over there. He has a mask on and he is taking honey from his hives. I will go ashore and ask him where Hoy is.'

'Be careful,' said Jorkel. 'We will have difficulty in getting to Hoy if there are only two of us left to work the ship.'

Sweyn waded ashore and said to the bee-keeper, 'Be good enough to tell us how we can recognize the island of Hoy.'

The man took off his mask and replied courteously that they would have to sail west between the islands until they reached the open ocean, and then keeping the coast of Hrossey on the port side and sailing south they would see in the distance two blue hills rising out of the sea. These blue hills were Hoy.

Sweyn thanked him and asked if he was getting plenty of honey.

The man replied that it was a bad year for honey. The bees had been as dull as the weather.

'Still,' the bee-keeper said, 'the next comb I take from the hive will be a gift for you.'

Sweyn was deeply touched by the courtesy and kindness of the bee-keeper.

It happened that as the man was bending over the hive, a bee came on the wind and settled on his neck and stung him.

The bee-keeper gave a cry of annoyance and shook off the bee.

Sweyn was angry at the way the insects repaid with ingratitude the gentleness of the Orkney bee-keeper. He suddenly brought his axe down on the hive and clove it in two.

Jorkel and Valt were watching from the ship, and they saw Sweyn run screaming round the island with a cloud of bees after him. It was as if he was being pelted with hot sharp sonorous hail stones.

Sweyn ran down into the ebb and covered himself with seaweed.

When Jorkel and Valt reached him, he told them where Hoy was. Then his face turned blind and blue and swollen and he died.

*

Jorkel and Valt got horses at a farm called the Bu in Hoy and rode between the two hills till they came to a place called Rackwick. There was a farm there and five men were working in the hayfield. It was a warm bright day, and the faces of the labourers shone with sweat.

Jorkel asked them if a man called Arkol lived nearby.

'Arkol is the grieve at this farm,' said one of the labourers, 'but he often sleeps late.'

'We work in the daytime,' said another, 'but Arkol does most of his labouring at night.'

'Arkol is a great man for the women,' said a third, and winked.

Jorkel said he thought that would be the man they were looking for.

Presently the labourers stopped to rest and they invited Jorkel and Valt to share their bread and ale. They sat under a wall where there was shadow and Valt told all that had happened to them from the time they left Bergen. But Jorkel sat quietly and seemed preoccupied. They noticed too that he did not eat or drink much.

'Who is the owner of this farm?' said Valt when he had finished his story of the voyage.

The labourers said the farmer in Rackwick was a man called John. They spoke highly of him. He was a good master to them.

Just then a man with a dark beard crossed the field. He ordered the labourers to resume their work, and then looked suspiciously at Jorkel and Valt. They were rather scruffy and dirty after their voyage.

Jorkel asked him if his name was Arkol Dagson.

The man yawned once or twice and said that it was.

'In that case,' said Jorkel, 'I must tell you that my sister Ingirid in Bergen bore you a son at the beginning of June.'

Arkol made no answer but yawned again. Then he laughed.

'And I want to know,' said Jorkel, 'if you will pay for the fostering of the child.'

Arkol said he would not discuss so intimate a matter with two tramps. So far he had not been in the habit of paying for the fostering of any child that he had fathered, and he doubted whether it was wise to begin now, especially as Norway was so far away. Furthermore, he could hardly be expected to believe the unsupported testimony of two tramps, one of whom claimed to be Ingirid's brother. Ingirid had been a most lovely and gently reared girl, and Arkol did not think the scarecrow standing before him could really be the brother of such a delightful bedmate. Besides, he had been busy all night in another sweet bed, and now he was very tired, and he begged the two gentlemen of the roads to excuse him.

Jorkel said, 'Will you pay now for the fostering of your son?'

Arkol turned away and yawned.

Jorkel drove his dagger into Arkol's throat, so that he fell dead at once on the field.

The labourers jumped down from the haystack and ran at Jorkel and Valt with their forks.

'I wish the others were here now,' said Jorkel as he turned to face them. 'Now I would be glad to have Finn and Flan and Mund and Thord and Sweyn at my side.'

Valt was quickly pronged to death there, and though Jorkel defended himself well and was still on his feet when

John of Rackwick appeared on the scene, he was so
severely lacerated that he lay between life and death in
the farm for more than a week.

The three farm girls looked after him well till he
recovered. They hovered around him day and night with
oil and sweet water and beeswax.

On the day they took the last bandages from Jorkel's
arm, John of Rackwick came to him and said mildly,
'Arkol, my grieve, was in many ways an evil lecherous
man, and for that he must answer to a higher lord than the
Earl of Orkney or the King of Norway. But also he was a
loyal servant of mine, and because of that you must pay
me as compensation your ship that is anchored off
Selwick. You are welcome to stay here in Hoy, Jorkel,
for as long as you like. There is a small vacant croft on the
side of the hill that will support a cow and an ox and a few
sheep. It will be a tame life for a young man, but now you
are disabled because of the hay forks, and if you till your
field carefully nothing could be more pleasing to God.'

Jorkel accepted that offer. He lived there at Upland for
the rest of his life. In Orkney he was nicknamed 'Hayforks'. He put by a little money each harvest so that one
day he would be able to return to Norway, but the years
passed and he could never get a passage.

*

The summer before his death Jorkel went to Papa Westray
in a fishing boat. At the church there he inquired for
Thord, and presently Thord came out to meet him. They

were two old men now, bald and toothless. They embraced each other under the arch. They were like two boys laughing to each other over an immense distance, thin affectionate lost voices.

Jorkel took a purse from his belt and counted five pieces of silver into Thord's hand. 'I have been saving this money for forty years,' he said, 'so that some day I could go home to Norway. But it is too late. Who would know me in Bergen now? I should prepare, instead, for the last, longest journey. Will you arrange for Masses to be said in your church for Finn and Flan and Mund and Sweyn and Valt?'

Thord said that Masses would certainly be offered for those dead men and for Jorkel himself too. Then he embraced Jorkel and blessed him. Jorkel turned round. He was at peace. The long silver scars of the hayforks troubled his body no longer.

Half-way to the boat he turned back. He gave Thord another silver coin. 'Say a Mass for Arkol Dagson also,' he said.

They smiled at each other, crinkling their old eyes.